CHEROKEE
STONE

CHEROKEE PASSAGES BOOK TWO

CHEROKEE STONE

CHEROKEE PASSAGES BOOK TWO

REGINA McLEMORE

FIFE
PRESS

an imprint of

YOUNG DRAGONS PRESS

OGHMA

C R E A T I V E   M E D I A

Bentonville, Arkansas • Los Angeles, California
www.oghmacreative.com

Library of Congress Cataloging-in-Publication Data

Names: McLemore Regina, author
Title: Cherokee Stone/Regina McLemore | Cherokee Passages #2
Description: First Edition | Bentonville: Fife, 2021
Identifiers: LCCN: 2021940265 | ISBN: 978-1-63373-703-7 (hardcover) |
ISBN: 978-1-63373-704-4 (trade paperback) | ISBN: 978-1-63373-705-1 (eBook)
BISAC: YOUNG ADULT FICTION/People & Places/United States/Native American
YOUNG ADULT FICTION/Historical/United States/19th Century
LC record available at: https://lccn.loc.gov/2021940265

Fife Press hardcover edition August, 2021

Cover & Interior Design by Casey W. Cowan
Editing by Cyndy Prasse Miller, Bob Giel, & Dennis Doty

Published by Fife Press, an imprint of Young Dragons Press, a subsidiary of The Oghma Book Group. Find out more at www.oghmacreative.com

My second book, Cherokee Stone, is first dedicated to all of my Cherokee and white ancestors that I only know through family stories and genealogical research, especially Susie Christie Clay, Riley Clay, Anderson McClain, Edna Scott McClain, Robert Barton Philpott, Dewilder Woolard Philpott, Delia Wortman Scott, and Zachariah Scott. Some very creative variations of their stories can be found in Cherokee Clay and Cherokee Stone.

Of those in my living memory, I want to honor Mary Clay Philpott and E.C. Philpott, my paternal grandparents, whose experiences inspired the characters of Amelia and Michael. I also want to honor my mother and father, Juanita McClain Philpott and Gene Philpott, who bore a rather striking resemblance to the characters, Bonita and Clay.

Finally, I want to dedicate Cherokee Stone to the late Blanche McKee Steeley, my mother's sister-like cousin and our Scott family treasure. Blanche provided the pattern for Blythe and was my source for so many stories about the Scott and McClain families.

TABLE OF CONTENTS

ACKNOWLEDGEMENTS

I WANT TO THANK ALL my colleagues and friends who have supported and guided me on the way to becoming a published author. My fellow authors, including Chris Murphy, Renee La Viness, Bob Giel, and Dennis Doty have all given me the benefit of their expertise and insight. My history loving friends at the Depot and my SPLFS friends at the Stilwell Library, as well as my "forever friends," Susie Thompson and Brenda Swepston Brown, have always inspired me to keep on course. Of course, I can't leave out my granddaughters, Samantha and Abigail, who never fail to make their Nana smile.

I

LOSING

AMELIA

AS THE YEAR of 1899 drew to a close, Amelia's despair grew as she looked around the bare white walls that surrounded her. The Cherokee Girls Mission was clean and spacious but utterly void of the comfortable touches that made a place a home. When she thought of the warm, cozy cabin where she had spent the first six years of her life, her stomach and heart ached with pain. All she could do was to follow the advice of her only friend at the Mission, Sarah. Sarah advised her to smile a lot and speak very little, and any words spoken must be in English. Amelia became a mute observer of the strangers around her.

They were like perfect little dolls when the staff members, whom Amelia secretly called "witches," were present, speaking quietly in their flawless English. Only Amelia was different, and, because of that difference, she was singled-out by one of the older girls. Rosalie's waist-length dark brown hair, streaked with auburn highlights, light skin, and perfect figure attracted attention. Large, dazzling green eyes made her beautiful. Amelia had never seen an Indian with such eyes before and could hardly restrain herself from staring at Rosalie. The staring almost led to her downfall.

"What are you staring at, you little darkie?"

Amelia, detecting anger in Rosalie's voice, got the general gist of what Rosalie was saying and quickly looked away.

"I said what are you staring at? Are you dim-witted as well as ugly?" Rosalie's group jeered and pointed at her. "Ugly darkie! Stupid half-wit!"

Amelia closed her eyes, put her hands over her ears, doubling herself into a small, brown ball, pretending nothing was happening. Maybe they would soon tire of the game, go away, and leave her alone.

Rosalie screamed, "Make her look at me!"

Her cohorts pried Amelia's hands from her ears, lifting her into an upright position.

Amelia's eyes flashed open involuntarily as Rosalie struck her face with a hard slap.

"Stop it! Leave the poor child alone."

"Sure, Sarah. I didn't know you had a new baby. This one is not nearly as pretty as Leona, but maybe we'll get lucky, and this one will die, too."

"You better watch what you say, Rosalie. Somebody might get the idea you had something to do with Leona's death. Come along, Amelia. I have something to show you."

Reluctantly Rosalie and her companions parted, allowing Sarah and Amelia to leave the room. Walking away, Amelia heard the girls murmuring something in English. "What did they say, Sarah?"

"Something silly about conjuring us."

Amelia stopped walking and shivered. "Do you think they will?"

Putting her hands on Amelia's shoulders, Sarah looked into her eyes. "Don't be afraid of Rosalie. Her bark is a lot worse than her bite. Now, come on, it's time for more lessons."

Sarah led Amelia to her own favorite dreaming place, a large boulder nestled in a pine tree nest, on the side of a small hill, overlooking a gurgling, clear stream. This quiet, hidden place had become Amelia's school, a sanctuary where Cherokee was not taboo, at least for instructional purposes. Sarah began teaching Amelia the English names for some common Cherokee nouns soon after they met. In a few weeks they moved on to phrases, and now, after six months of instruction, Amelia could understand almost everything that was said to her and could speak in simple, complete English sentences.

As well as instructing Amelia in the English language, Sarah showed her how to braid her hair into tight braids and gave her a wide-brimmed hat to wear in the sun. This would guard Amelia's skin from turning "black" from the sun, since dark skin was shunned at the school. Perhaps, most importantly of all, Sarah taught Amelia to look without fear into the faces of those who spoke to her, even the witches.

"They are not really witches, you know. They are just white people, and some of them are harder to tolerate. The music teacher is rather sweet, but Matron can be a devil. Perhaps you are right, maybe she is a witch, but not the kind of witch you fear. Rosalie and her followers dream of being witches, but they aren't real ones. That's not to say Rosalie isn't wicked. I suspect she somehow caused Leona's death."

Amelia started to ask Sarah why she thought this, but talking about Rosalie always agitated her. She wanted to talk back when Rosalie or one of her followers called her names or gave her mean looks, but she didn't trust her English skills to say the right words. Someday Amelia would ask Sarah to tell her everything she suspected about Rosalie, and someday she would stand up for herself against Rosalie and her gang.

Amelia lived for the leisure time between supper and bedtime when she could slip away and see Sarah. Sometimes Sarah was detained by study or extra work and couldn't meet her. She usually signaled Amelia she wouldn't be there, like a simple note pressed into Amelia's hand at supper. Amelia went to the secret spot a few times without Sarah, but fear always drove her away. Only Sarah's presence made it a beautiful place. More and more, in her secret heart, she called Sarah "my sister."

Amelia's day began with her second favorite class, Arithmetic. It was the opposite of the shifting sands of her last and least favorite class, Grammar, where English words changed meaning with a change in pronunciation or spelling. Arithmetic was like concrete, and two plus two could be relied on to always equal four. She could tolerate Deportment, where the girls were taught the social niceties of educated women, because her favorite class soon followed. Understanding harmony and rhythm instinctively, Amelia excelled at Music.

With Sarah as her protector, Amelia acclimated quickly, and without the threat of persecution or punishment, she thrived, especially in Music. Delighting in the melodious harmony of girlish voices raised together in a sweet hymn, she could forget that she was different. Even when she didn't completely understand the words, Amelia found comfort in "It is Well with my Soul" and "Whispering Hope." Her clear, high, child's soprano caught the ear of Miss Jennings, the music teacher, and she favored Amelia with a smile and praise.

"That was lovely, Amelia."

Amelia looked over at Sarah to see her reaction to the compliment and smiled because Sarah beamed like a proud mother. As she turned back to her hymnal, Amelia glanced at Rosalie and caught a dagger-like stare.

Miss Jennings touched Amelia's shoulder as the girls were filing out to their next class. "Amelia, I need a helper to clean and straighten the conservatory every day. Would you be interested?"

"Oh, yes, ma'am."

Amelia was thrilled to be rescued from her station as a kitchen aide. She was tired of peeling potatoes, scrubbing the floor, and washing greasy pots and pans over and over. She cringed each time Miss Jones said, "These still aren't clean."

Miss Jennings' smile and words warmed Amelia's heart. "All right then. I'll see you this afternoon."

Reporting to Miss Jennings, she was told "watch for a bit and then you can finish what I start." Miss Jennings quickly demonstrated how the hardwood floor should be swept, mopped, and buffed. Each piece of furniture must be dusted thoroughly, and each hymnal and music book dusted off and returned to the proper place. Even the sweet Miss Jennings followed the white notion of, "A place for everything, and everything in its place."

The two hours of work moved fast and proved enjoyable, especially when Amelia cleaned the keys of the huge, oak, upright piano. Her fingers skipping over the magical black and white keys, each key sang its own unique song. In time, Amelia learned to pick-out small melodies, playing and singing quietly to herself. Although she could not get all the underlying chords, Amelia could play a recognizable "Amazing Grace," "Whispering Hope," and even, "A Mighty Fortress Is Our God." Losing herself in the rhapsody of music, she smiled almost as much as when she was with Sarah.

FOUR YEARS PASSED quietly and happily for Amelia. Although her father wrote to her occasionally and always sent her money at Christmas, he rarely came to see her. She barely remembered her life before coming to the Mission. Her mother existed as a shadowy dream figure, and her father and brothers appeared only slightly more substantial. Yes, she still considered Sarah to be like an older, wiser sister, but she now had other friends, some older or younger than she. Like a butterfly emerging from a cocoon, Amelia had metamorphosed. She was no longer the thin, short, nervous child who kept her eyes focused on the ground. Even though she was still one of the shortest girls at the Mission, she had grown several inches and maintained a normal weight. Her eyes shone bright and sparkling, her hair a shiny black cascade when loosened from her braids, her skin smooth and a pleasing beige color. No one called her ugly anymore, and her lilting girlish voice was deepening into a rich contralto, much praised by Miss Jennings. Life would be perfect if not for Rosalie and her band focusing their energy on terrorizing the younger girls. One such incident almost ended in tragedy for Amelia's friend.

Rachael Threestar, a dark-skinned eight-year-old, was only at the mission for a few hours before she was befriended by Amelia. Due to a lack of space, Rachael was assigned to sleep in the intermediate room.

The other four girls rooming with Amelia protested and complained. "Why did they put the new one in with us?"

"She's just a little girl."

"It's already too crowded in here."

"Well, she can't sleep by me, because I almost hit the wall now when I just turn over."

Amelia, sympathizing with the sad-eyed stranger, welcomed her. "There's a little space by my bed. Move your cot here and sleep by me."

This act of kindness earned Amelia a steadfast friend, and Rachael began following Amelia around like a little pup. Amelia enjoyed the attention, but soon started fretting about seldom getting away from Rachael to see Sarah. Even though, more often than not, Sarah canceled their meetings, Amelia's heart yearned for Sarah and the friendship they once shared. Her spirits soared one sunny Friday when Sarah didn't pass her the usual note of excuse.

As soon as she could leave the supper table, Amelia told Rachael she had to visit the privy. She ducked behind the outhouse, running up the path to the secret spot. Poised to climb the hill, Amelia stopped, her keen ears picking up footsteps. Hiding behind a large oak tree, she saw Rachael stumbling over the unfamiliar terrain.

"Please, Amelia. I know you're close by. You might be mad that I followed you, but if you leave me here, I'll never find my way back."

Amelia had one foot out of hiding when a familiar voice whined. "Please, Amelia, don't leave me. I'm so scared, I might pee my drawers."

Amelia quickly ducked back behind the tree. Taunting laughter rang out. Rachael had also been followed—by Rosalie and company. The four girls quickly surrounded their prey. Amelia's eyes doubled in size, seeing Rosalie smoking a homemade cigarette. If Matron knew about her smoking, Rosalie would be put out on the road. Yet Rosalie showed no fear of Rachael tattling on her, and this accelerated Amelia's fear level.

Rosalie blew a smoke ring into Rachael's ashen face. "Been conjurin' you for six days, girl, and you know what that means. I've got some of your hair and fingernails right here in this bag. I already have your soul, and now I've come to claim your body."

At the sight of her hair and nail clippings, Rachael nearly fainted, falling at the feet of her tormentors. She whispered something in Cherokee so softly that Amelia barely heard her pleading for her life. Rosalie blew smoke rings around Rachael's head and cackled.

"It won't do you any good to call on the Creator or the whites' Jesus. Leona did both, but she still died."

Now, Amelia knew what had happened to Leona, and she knew what was going to happen to Rachael if she didn't interfere. But what could she do against four mean girls?

She remained frozen behind a tree as Rosalie tormented her friend. "Can't you feel your heart beatin' faster and faster? It's going to explode in a minute just like Leona's heart."

Amelia cringed as she watched a re-creation of Leona's murder. Rachael's breathing grew loud and rasping, and she clutched at her heart with small trembling hands. Amelia had to act—now. She picked up a rock to throw at Rosalie the same second another familiar voice rang out.

"You stupid fools! What are you trying to do to this child? Get up, Rachael, and come to me. There's nothing to be afraid of."

Sarah reached out to help Rachael up, turning her back on Rosalie as she did. Only Amelia could see the knife behind Rosalie's back, raised to attack Sarah. Without stopping to think, she stepped from behind the tree, bringing the large rock crashing down on Rosalie's skull, seconds before she would have stabbed Sarah.

Time froze as everyone watched the blood gushing from Rosalie's head. Rosalie fell to the ground as her friends turned to run away.

Sarah took charge. "Girls, hurry, tear up your petticoats and make bandages. Amelia, get some water from the stream. Here, take our drinking jug." Sarah attempted to staunch the blood flow with her fingers while everyone followed orders.

After the flow nearly stopped, Sarah bandaged Rosalie's head and issued a stern warning. "This is what happened today. Rosalie cut her head when she fell on an unfamiliar path. If I ever hear anything different, I will go to Matron and tell her everything you girls have been up to, and I will take this cigarette as evidence. I will include the part about your involvement in Leona's death. You know she will believe me, don't you?"

"Yes, Sarah."

"Oh, and when Rosalie comes to, tell her what happened today. Be sure to tell her everything Amelia did and tell her if she tries to hurt Amelia or her friends again, Amelia will kill her."

"Of course, Sarah." Rosalie's friends carried her gingerly down the path to the front door of the mission while the other three girls scurried through the back door.

True peace finally reigned at the school, but Amelia never had Sarah all to herself again. Since she had been named as an assistant teacher for the youngest girls, Sarah's time was taken up with classroom duties. If she agreed to do anything with Amelia, Rachael always accompanied them, even to their secret place. Sarah didn't seem to mind, laughing at Rachael's silly jokes and mischievous ways. Amelia, naturally quiet and reserved, was a little jealous. On one occasion Rachael wouldn't quit teasing about the delivery boy who brought provisions to the school, and his habit of winking at Amelia. Amelia sat brooding for some time, ignoring the teasing.

When Rachael continued, she suddenly exploded. "Would you stop it? I am so sick of hearing about that stupid delivery boy!"

Sarah chuckled, wagging her finger. "Amelia, Rachael is only teasing you a little. You really must learn to take a joke."

Amelia plugged her ears with her fingers. "I don't want to learn how. Jokes are stupid." She didn't speak for the rest of the day.

YET, EVEN WITH their disagreements, things went along pretty smoothly until Amelia's eleventh birthday. It started out so nicely. Sarah arranged a real birthday party for Amelia. In the past,

Sarah had always baked her favorite cake, chocolate, and they had their own private birthday party. Sarah always made or bought her a small inexpensive present. When she was younger, Sarah made her toys, like the beautiful rag doll that she had named Saralyn because it seemed like a regal form of Sarah's name. But last year, saying Amelia was too old for toys, Sarah gave her a dress that she had sewn herself. Amelia fought to hide her disappointment.

This year, most of the girls, even two members of Rosalie's crew, gathered around the table and sang, "Happy Birthday" to Amelia. Not only did Sarah bake a big cake, but she made a special treat, homemade vanilla ice cream. Several of the girls gave Amelia presents, ranging from colorful hair ribbons to a book of famous paintings, Sarah's present to Amelia. Amelia beamed with happiness, eagerly untying each newspaper-wrapped parcel, but then, after each gift was exclaimed over and each giver thanked, the grand finale occurred.

Miss Jennings, accompanied by a tall, slender, blond-haired stranger, came into the room, bending down and kissing Amelia's forehead. "Amelia, I wouldn't miss your birthday party for anything. Here's a little gift from me."

She offered Amelia a delicate lace handkerchief with its ends tied together, preventing a round object from falling from its center. Amelia was so excited she couldn't untie the knot to see what was inside, and the stranger kindly offered his assistance. "Here, missy, let me see if I can help you with that."

As long, strong fingers untied the hard knot, Miss Jennings chuckled. "My goodness, where are my manners? Girls, let me introduce you to my younger brother, Thomas Jennings. He is going to stay with me for a while until he can find a position and residence in town."

After each girl politely introduced herself, Thomas Jennings smiled and handed Amelia the handkerchief and a shiny silver dollar.

Amelia gasped with delight. She had never had so much money before. In an unusual display of affection, she ran over to Miss Jennings and hugged her around the waist. "Oh, thank you, Miss Jennings!"

"You're welcome, child. Perhaps Sarah and Thomas could take you to town to spend your money. You may borrow my wagon if you wish. I think you two have met, haven't you?"

At that moment, catching the look that passed between Sarah and Thomas Jennings, Amelia realized not only had they met, but something more than mere acquaintanceship existed between them. She sensed her life with Sarah had changed forever.

THE TREAT OF going to town seemed diminished somehow, but Sarah insisted, and Amelia found herself sitting in the back of Miss Jennings' smart carriage, drawn by two handsome sorrels. Sarah and Thomas Jennings sat close together on the front seat, murmuring conversation she couldn't hear over the sound of the horses' trotting. But it was a beautiful June morning, and Amelia's eager eyes took in the beauty around her. It had been a rainy spring, and the lush greenness of the foliage and the glory of the wild Indian paintbrush, bright trumpet vine, fragrant honeysuckle, and other flowers Amelia couldn't name, filled her with delight. July would bring the sweat-producing, body-draining humidity which would drive everyone to seek shade, but for now Amelia thanked God for June.

She tapped Sarah on the shoulder to get her attention. "Let me get out and walk the rest of the way. It's just a mile or so to town,"

"Oh, all right, but see you don't stray off the road and get into a bunch of ticks and chiggers. We'll meet you on the courthouse lawn."

Amelia hopped down from the wagon, smelling and picking the most fragrant and most colorful flowers, and then binding them together with her new handkerchief. She grinned when she glimpsed blackberries growing a few feet off the road. Waiting until Sarah was out of sight, she left the road to investigate and spent several delightful minutes popping the tart, red berries into her mouth. They wouldn't fully ripen until late June, but she preferred them slightly tart. She wished for something to put them in so she could gather some to take back to cook. Her mouth salivated at the image of a fresh, warm, blackberry cobbler with some of the delicious ice cream. Remembering Sarah's admonition to stay on the road and realizing a bundle of blackberries would be proof of her disobedience, she contented herself with eating until she was stuffed. When Amelia's appetite was staved, she looked down at her hands and noticed they were stained with the tell-tale dark purple juice. Now, there was likely no way to avoid a scolding. Spying a little stream just a short distance away, Amelia proceeded cautiously into the woods, being on watch for snakes.

Maybe that was the reason she didn't see the old black lady, sitting on a big rock by the water until she was almost on her. Amelia gasped with surprise. Before her sat what must be the darkest Indian in the world.

"What's the matter, girlie, ain't you never seen the likes of old Annie before? I won't hurt you 'cause I wants to help you. Come here, child, and I'll worsh you up and mebee tell yur fortune if you has any money."

Amelia had been admonished to never talk to strangers, but this old lady seemed friendly enough. Never having seen a Negro, but having read about them, she now realized she was looking at one. She was intrigued by the idea of getting her fortune authentically read. Some of the girls claimed they could read fortunes by examining the coffee grounds left in an empty cup. A lot of it seemed repetitious, the usual stuff about getting married and living in a big house. Rosalie was supposed to be the best, and some girls swore what she foretold came true. Amelia remained leery of what Rosalie might say about her future.

Annie took a small vial from her neck, pouring a substance from it onto Amelia's hands, and rinsing them in the clear, cool water. Whatever the mystery substance was, it took most of the blackberry stains from her hands. Leading Amelia back to the large rock where she had been seated, Annie motioned for Amelia to sit beside her. She reached into a pocket and produced a deck of tattered cards. Amelia's mind flashed back to one of Reverend Spencer's sermons. He had called cards "the Devil's own invention." She considered leaving, but the fascination of the mysterious old lady and her red and black snares kept her captive.

"This is you, honey, the Queen of Clubs because of yur dark hair and complexion. Now give me two bits, and I'll very gladly tell yur true fortune."

"All I have is this silver dollar. Can you give me change?"

"Sure nuff. Here you go."

Annie gave her some silver coins and copper pennies, but Amelia was too excited to count the change.

Handing the deck to Amelia, she said, "Cut the deck, honey, into three piles and make a wish on the last pile."

Amelia did as she was told, wishing that Sarah would forget about Thomas Jennings, and Annie took the top card off each of the piles, placing them beside the Queen of Clubs.

Muttering to herself, Annie shuffled the deck, laid down some cards, and gradually picked up more until seven cards lay before Amelia. "You don't get yur wish cause the wish card ain't come up, but you is goin' to get a heap of good things and some bad, too, just like life. I know for a fact you's goin' to get married, have lots of pretty babies, and live in a big house."

Annie paused, pointing to the Jack of Diamonds. "For a fact, you will marry this here sandy-haired, blue-eyed Jack, and he'll have a proud past. If you wants to know more, it'll cost you the rest o' that silver dollar."

Amelia stared at Annie, considering the notion of squandering all her money for a fortune that sounded like one that the mission girls told, except for that last part about the Jack of Diamonds. "No, thank you, ma'am. I have to save some money for town, but maybe I'll come back and see you again sometime."

Annie scowled and filled her corncob pipe with tobacco. "Suit yurself, then."

Amelia set off running as fast as her short legs would carry her. She knew it was getting late, and Sarah would be worried. Approaching the courthouse lawn, she saw Sarah looking down the road with an anxious expression on her face.

Catching sight of Amelia, the worried look changed to an annoyed expression. Walking out to meet Amelia, she exclaimed, "It's about time you got here. I sent Tom to look in all of the stores for you, and I was thinking about going to the sheriff's office next."

Amelia smirked at her use of "Tom" instead of Mr. Jennings.

"Where have you been?"

"Oh, Sarah, I had the most exciting adventure. I met this old Negro lady, and she told my fortune. Oh, and here's some flowers I picked for you."

Sarah took the bouquet, shook her head, and rolled her eyes. "Amelia, I'm disappointed in you. Haven't I told you that fortunetelling is superstitious nonsense? How much did she charge you? Let me see how much money you have left out of your silver dollar?"

Amelia ashamedly held out the change while Sarah counted it.

"Amelia, that old fraud cheated you out of almost sixty cents! Now you don't have enough money to buy hardly anything. Oh, well, no use crying over spilled milk. Maybe we can buy some material and make you a new dress."

"But I don't want a dress, Sarah. I want a harmonica."

"Well, it's your money, but your Sunday dress is faded and worn, and I don't know why you want to waste your money on play pretties."

Amelia stood firm. "You're right. It's my money."

They met Thomas coming out of the Aiden General Store as they were going in.

He grinned and winked at Amelia. "The prodigal has returned I see."

"Yes, with no apologies for her lateness."

"I'm sorry, Sarah, but can we just look around? I've only been in here a few times, but I remember where most things are. See, here's the harmonica I've been wanting, and it's only twenty cents. Here's twenty cents you can use to buy me something useful. Then I can get us all a peppermint stick and some lemon drops."

Thomas laughed as he squeezed Sarah's waist. "No candy for me, sugar. I've got all the sweets I want right here."

Sarah frowned and scolded him. "Tom! Not in front of the child!"

Thomas's hand remained around Sarah's waist.

Amelia paid for her purchases and stuck the extra peppermint sticks and lemon drops in her sack to take back to share with Rachael. She stood quietly watching as Sarah spotted some red silk material to admire and gush over.

Thomas directed the clerk to "wrap up enough of that red silk to make my pretty lady a dress." In an undertone, he added, "I'll be expecting Santa to give me a nice present in exchange for that silk." He winked, and Sarah blushed.

Amelia practiced on her harmonica all the way home. She was glad she had something to do, so she could ignore what was going on in the driver's seat. She heard Sarah giggle and say, "Tom, stop that!" several times, and she saw Thomas Jennings tilt a brown bag to his mouth and take a swig of something liquid.

WHEN THEY REACHED the school, it was twilight, and Thomas stopped the wagon in front of the gates. "Time to go in, little papoose."

Sarah snickered and held out a package. "Wait, Amelia, here's some white gloves I bought you with your twenty cents. You can wear them to church on Sunday."

Amelia took the gloves and mumbled her thanks as she opened the gates.

Once in her room, she threw the gloves in her drawer of the large wooden dresser that everyone shared.

Rachael was overjoyed to share the candy with Amelia. Candy was usually only seen at Christmas time at the school. She giggled when Amelia played her harmonica. "You sound like a scalded cat."

Ignoring her, Amelia played until bedtime, finding it hard to even play a simple tune. The piano was much easier.

The next morning and for many mornings and evenings after, Sarah surrounded herself with the older girls. They laughed and talked about their beaus whenever they had a spare minute from their chores. They would run off any of the younger girls who came around them, scolding them with, "Go away, little girls. This is women's talk."

The first time this happened to Amelia, she looked at Sarah to see if she would come to her defense as she had always done, but she only grinned and said nothing.

For several days, Amelia had been watching the trees for signs of the approaching fall, her favorite season. Finally, one cool evening, she went to bed and awoke to a beautiful Ozark autumn. A heavy frost lay on the ground like a diamond comforter, and the maples surrounding the school appeared to have been dipped in a gigantic gallon of paint. The riotous red and gold leaves lent an appearance of festivity to the plain, white clapboard mission. Touching the cold, wet glass on the big window by her bed, she gleefully wrote, A-m-e-l-i-a. Throwing it wide open, she took a deep gulp of the crisp autumn air. What a beautiful morning! From the downstairs kitchen wafted a promise of buttermilk biscuits, cream gravy, fresh ham, and fried eggs. The fragrant aroma filled her nostrils, and her stomach growled in hungry anticipation.

Rachael's soft snores indicated she was still fast asleep with flannel sheets and patchwork quilts pulled to her chin, and Amelia couldn't resist pulling them off. She shouted, "Get up, lazy bones! Daylight's burning, and it's Saturday."

When Rachael heard the word "Saturday," she sprang from her bed like a jack-in-the-box. "I almost forgot, Amelia! Today's the day Mr. Jennings is going to take us all to town!"

Amelia and Rachael hurried to the washroom, taking a quick sponge bath and putting on fresh white blouses and their usual navy broadcloth jumpers. They brushed out the tangles in their long, wild manes, helping each other with the daily hair braiding, and running downstairs for a delicious hot breakfast.

Thomas Jennings and Sarah each drove a large buckboard, filled to capacity with giggly, excited girls. Amelia felt reassured when she saw the large crowd of girls. They wouldn't act silly with so many witnesses to report their bad behavior.

SARAH AND THOMAS bought the necessary supplies while the girls spent their hoarded pennies. Thomas bought them all a peppermint stick, which Amelia thought was nice of him. She knew he couldn't make much money being a hired hand for the Mission, even if he lived there in a small house with his sister.

After returning to the Mission and eating supper, Amelia realized she still had about an hour before sunset. That was enough time for a quick walk to Amelia's new secret place, if she could get shed of Rachael for a few minutes. Fortunately, as soon as they finished eating, Emily, one of the younger girls, asked Rachael and Amelia to come to her room for a tea party. Offering a headache as an excuse, she grabbed the flour sack where she stored her harmonica and other items and left by the back door.

A SHORT DISTANCE from the secret place she and Sarah once shared, Amelia set up a new place. Smiling in anticipation, she took out the little braided rug she could store deep in the hollow of an old oak tree. Sitting down on the rug under the tree, she began playing her harmonica. She was so intent on playing "Darling Clementine" that she didn't realize someone was behind her until she heard a cough.

"Why, papoose, that sounds right pretty, almost as pretty as you look. You're getting to be a real nice-looking young lady, aren't you?"

"Thank you, Mr. Jennings. I'm sorry I can't stay and talk to you, but it will soon be dark, and I must leave." Amelia cleaned off the harmonica and put it in her flour sack.

"Oh, come on, papoose. Dark's not for another thirty minutes or so, and that gives us plenty of time to talk. How old are you now, honey?"

"I'm eleven. Would you please move your arm away?"

Jennings had lowered himself to sit beside her, carelessly throwing his arm around her shoulders. "But, sweetie, I'm lonesome for female company, and you're definitely a female." He lowered his hand to touch Amelia's budding breasts.

Angered, Amelia shouted, "Stop that!" and tried to get to her feet.

Jennings threw her down to the ground and pressed his hard, cruel, male lips against her soft childish mouth.

Amelia slapped and kicked but could do nothing against his man's strength. Closing her eyes, she tried to wish him away.

When his strong, whiskey breath nearly gagged her, she opened her eyes to discover his bloodshot blue eyes were staring at her but not seeing her. She tried to rise, but he pushed her back down, so she closed her eyes again and waited for the unknown.

Jennings ripped her petticoat and pantaloons, but the tough broadcloth jumper held together. Jennings cursed and took out his knife to cut her clothes from her.

She grabbed at the knife but only succeeded in cutting her hand. She tried to curl herself into a little ball to hide her near nakedness.

Sarah suddenly loomed over them. "What's going on here?"

Jennings quickly stood to his feet, brushing himself off. "This little harlot followed me out to the woods, stripped herself naked, and begged me to fornicate with her. I was trying to get her to put her clothes on and go back to the school."

Amelia lay motionless, still in a state of shock.

"Get up, you shameless hussy, and don't let me ever catch you close to my man again!"

She found herself speaking in Cherokee to Sarah, trying to explain what had happened. Amelia's innocence kept her from knowing exactly what Jennings had planned to do to her, but she told Sarah about his holding her to the ground and cutting her clothes off.

Sarah waved away her words. "Didn't I tell you never to speak Cherokee to me again? I won't tell Matron about what you tried to do tonight, but I will certainly tell her about your breaking the language rule. I don't know you anymore."

THEY LEFT THE shattered child on the cold ground, trying to gather what remained of her clothes.

She finally managed to tie the braided rug around her waist, stumbling off to the backdoor of the school. Washing and bandaging her bloody hand, hiding her ragged clothes under her bed, she put on a fresh nightgown, and crawled into bed. She put a pillow over her head and pretended to be asleep when Rachael and the rest of her roommates arrived. She remained in bed until all the lights were out, and she knew they were asleep. Amelia rose from her bed and made her way to the large pantry of the kitchen.

There, behind the lard cans and the sacks of flour, she cried until there were no more tears in her, and, for the first time, she built the wall. The wall would shield Amelia from those who sought to hurt her, the same wall which would hide her heart from any daring to love her.

When she emerged from her cave several hours later, Amelia appeared dry-eyed and as impassive as a cold, hard stone.

THE NEXT MORNING her small hand trembled a little when Miss Franklin bent over Amelia's slate to tell her Matron wanted to see her immediately.

The other girls stared and murmured their astonishment. Amelia heard one comment. "Amelia never gets in trouble."

She walked down the long corridor, steeling herself to deal with Sarah's betrayal and the harsh punishment she would soon undergo.

Matron didn't look so frightening when she knocked on the door, obeyed the command to "come in," and timidly approached the big mahogany desk. Amelia's heart hammered when the tall muscular woman stood up and raised her cane. Amelia knew no questions would be asked because her guilt was already proven by Sarah's testimony against her.

"You have been speaking with a heathen tongue again. You have been fairly warned about the consequences of breaking our rules, yet you rebelliously disobey. Pull your jumper off and lean over that chair."

It took Amelia a few minutes to get the jumper off. It was an old one, and a bit tight. Jennings had destroyed her new jumper. After folding and placing it in the chair she braced herself on, she took a deep breath. She closed her eyes and attempted to erect the wall of nonfeeling.

Matron was getting impatient. "Don't take all day about it."

The rod came across Amelia's back and legs again and again, and yet she didn't cry.

The matron stopped swinging and glared at her for several minutes. "You are a cold creature. Take off your blouse."

Amelia obeyed, standing calmly in her petticoat and drawers. This time the rod came across her back with such a force that it broke in two.

The matron flung away the broken pieces in disgust, "Leave, you evil child. No supper for you tonight, and I will not be so easy on you if you ever come back to me again." After this last remark, she took a handkerchief from her pocket and wiped her perspiring brow.

II

LEAVE

TAKING

THE MORNING AFTER the beating, the pain she endured forced Amelia to leave her warm bed hours before breakfast time. No matter how many pillows and blankets she placed under the wounds on her body, no matter how often she changed positions, Amelia found no comfort in sleep. She arose from her bed like an old, arthritic lady, coming close to fainting when she took her first step. Amelia shook her head to clear it and concentrated, working to muster the strength to get ready for school. Dressing herself and braiding her hair seemed to take hours. When she was finished, she took slow baby steps all the way to the outhouse. After several attempts, and many tears, she lowered herself to urinate. The walk back to the school was just as hard, and she stopped several times before reaching the back door.

Once there, she paused, gathering strength before setting off for the washroom. By the time she left there, the kitchen staff was preparing breakfast, and her stomach growled to remind her of its hungry state. If she sat in the common area waiting for breakfast, she might get in trouble, so she shuffled her way outside again. Finding a bench in a quiet corner of the backyard, she seated herself and waited.

Several minutes passed, and Amelia spent the time reflecting on what she must do to get through the upcoming school day. Hearing the murmur of young voices, she arose, walking painfully back to the dining hall. Waiting in line for her plate to be filled, she heard whispers and stifled laughter. Everyone knew what had happened to her, and now they were laughing at her. She averted her eyes, walking past the table where Sarah sat with the older girls, taking a seat beside Rachael and a group of the younger girls.

Rachael's sad eyes reflected her concern. "How are you feeling, Amelia? I heard you groaning in your sleep last night."

"I am doing all right. Thanks for asking." Amelia busied herself with buttering toast and shoveling oatmeal into her mouth, while Rachael turned to her best friend, Emily, and they chatted and giggled until a nearby teacher shushed them. Amelia quickly cleared her plate and stood up to take it to the kitchen area for washing.

When she reached the kitchen, Miss Jones put out her hand to stop her. "Amelia, has anyone told you that you will be working for me again, starting this morning?"

Amelia kept her face emotionless. "No, no one has told me. What do you want me to do?"

"Put on an apron and start washing dishes. You will be doing this every morning, and you will come back during your work period and help clean the kitchen and prepare food for tomorrow, just like you used to do."

"All right." At first Amelia resented working in the kitchen again, but as she scrubbed each dirty dish and utensil, she discovered one small bright note. Working in the kitchen, she didn't have to listen to the other girls giggle and whisper about her.

Once, on her way to her first class, she encountered Rosalie and her best friend, Verna, blocking the hallway. Amelia allowed the hatred in her heart to manifest in her face, and Verna ran away in terror. When Rosalie loitered behind, Amelia put all her strength into a hard shove, which put Rosalie on her back, staring up in astonishment.

Amelia smiled when she heard an onlooker say, "Did you see that?" The crowd parted, and Amelia walked to class, unimpeded.

In the days ahead, Amelia's new coping mechanisms worked well. As much as possible, she avoided the presence of the other girls, spending her leisure time in walking to a favorite quiet place where she could read or play her harmonica in solitude. One time, when she accidentally stumbled upon Sarah and Thomas, naked in a clump of bushes, she averted her eyes and ran off before they spotted her.

She never initiated conversation with anyone, but she did speak when spoken to, howbeit in short sentences. Rachael and Emily tried to draw her into their talk and play, and she was never rude to them. However, even when she was in the middle of talking to them, her eyes and thoughts were focused elsewhere.

Rachael noticed the change in Amelia's behavior. "What's wrong, Amelia? You never talk to Sarah anymore, and you barely talk to Emily or me."

"Nothing's wrong. I just don't have much to say these days, and Sarah has new friends now."

"Well, I'm sorry Sarah is acting that way, but you know I will always be your friend."

For once, Amelia looked Rachael in the face and gave her a warm smile. "I know you have, and I will always love you for it. Now, excuse me, but I need to finish a letter to my pa." Picking up the stationery, fountain pen, and bottle of ink she had purchased during her last trip to town, she moved to a quiet study area located in the common room. Looking around to make sure no one was spying on her, she wrote,

Dear Pa,

I hope this letter finds you and my brothers well. I am doing all right, but I have a favor to ask you. Would you please come here and take me home? I have been here for six years, and I would really like to have Christmas with you, John, and Will this year. Maybe I could stay after Christmas, too. Please write back soon. Thank you.

Sincerely,
Your daughter, Amelia Star Clay

Two weeks later, an excited Amelia ripped open a rare letter from home. Inside the letter was another smaller envelope, which she removed. Hearing a knock, she quickly crammed everything into the pocket of her jumper and opened the door to her room.

Rachel reached in and grabbed her hand. "Come on, Amelia! Mister Jennings and Sarah are taking all of us on a nature hike through the woods."

Amelia pulled away. "Sorry, Rachael. I have a cold, so I better stay out of the woods today."

"Oh, that's too bad. Do you want me to look for some pretty leaves and rocks for your collection?"

"Sure. I would appreciate that."

"I will do that then. See you later."

"All right." Amelia removed the letter from her pocket and sat down on her bed to read it.

Dear Milly,

We are all fine and hope you are the same. I am sorry, but I can't bring you home. I promised your mother that I would take good care of you, and the Mission is teaching you how to be a real lady like your mother. Here is a silver dollar to spend on one of your trips to the store. When it gets closer to Christmas, I will send you more money.

With my love,
Pa

Amelia unwrapped the silver dollar and threw it in her dresser drawer. Tears streaming down her face, she tore the letter into a hundred tiny pieces and threw them out the window.

Less than two years after his attack on Amelia, Thomas' sister found him attempting to trap young Emily in the Mission barn. Emily told Rachael what had happened, and Rachael ran to relay the scandalous news to Amelia. "You never will believe what just happened!"

Hearing the excitement in Rachael's voice, Amelia put down her book to listen. "What's that?"

"Emily told me Thomas Jennings threw her down in the barn, but his sister made him let her back up."

Amelia's heart sped up. "Did he hurt her?"

"No, just scared her. But he won't scare anybody else because Miss Jennings ran him off!"

"Hmmm…wonder what Sarah thought about that?"

"I don't know, but Miss Jennings is talking to her right now."

Amelia never knew what Miss Jennings had said to Sarah, but she must have believed her because, one day, she pressed a note in Amelia's hand as she was leaving her deportment class. Later that day, Amelia read it.

Dear Amelia,

You were right about Thomas. He is a terrible man. He tried to rape Emily, and he tried to rape you. I am sorry I didn't believe you. If you ever want to talk, just let me know.

Sincerely,
Your friend,
Sarah

AMELIA NEVER APPROACHED Sarah, nor did she respond to Sarah's greetings or smiles. Finally, one day, Sarah followed her to one of her favorite spots. Amelia was practicing her harmonica and didn't hear Sarah's approach.

"Amelia, we need to talk."

Amelia lowered her harmonica and turned expressionless eyes toward Sarah. "We have nothing to talk about."

"Yes, we do. I want to apologize to you for the way I have treated you. I would like for us to be friends again."

Amelia lowered her head for a minute before facing Sarah as she rose to her feet. "Thank you for the apology, but we can never be friends again. Goodbye."

Sarah never tried to approach her again, but she always smiled and waved when she encountered Amelia around the school. Amelia returned the waves but not the smiles.

WHEN AMELIA'S FATHER took her away from the Mission two years later, he found a quiet, sullen girl, standing on the front steps. Beside her was a pretty, younger girl who smiled up at him.

"Hello, Mister Clay. I'm Amelia's friend, Rachael."

"Well, hello, Rachael. I'm glad to meet you."

"Glad to meet you, too. I just wanted to tell Amelia goodbye before she leaves." She sobbed and clutched Amelia tightly. "I will miss you so!"

Amelia removed herself from the embrace and awkwardly patted Rachael's shoulder. "I will miss you, too, Rachael. I left a box of old dolls and other things someone gave me in our closet. Anything you don't want you can give to someone else."

"Thanks. Here's a little something to remember me by." Rachael handed Amelia a home-made card and a satin sachet bag filled with crushed wildflowers.

Amelia examined the card and sniffed the bag. "That smells lovely, and the card is really pretty. Thank you, Rachael."

Rachael hugged her again. "Goodbye. Don't forget to write." She walked away with tears in her eyes.

"I'll try not to forget. Goodbye."

ON THE WAY home, Pa asked her. "What ever happened to that Sarah girl you used to mention in your letters?"

"She graduated a while back and became a full-time teacher at the Mission."

When Amelia walked into her old room, she threw the sachet and card into the bottom drawer of the empty pine dresser. She resolved to forget Rachael as well as all the others. That part of her life was over, and she would seldom speak of it in her later years. For now, there was only work and a quiet existence with her family.

Learning to cook and clean for her father and her brother, John, was simple compared to the hard drudgery she was accustomed to in the kitchen of the school. William had married and moved to the far corner of the Clay allotment. When John first told her about the marriage, Amelia couldn't help but question him. "Who would want to marry Will? All he ever did was hunt and fish with his Keetoowah friends, and he barely talked to us, much less a girl."

John's right hand couldn't hide the smirk that covered his face. "Don't think him and Penelope did much talkin', which is why she claims Rosemary came early."

Amelia's top lip curled in disgust. "But why Penelope Drake?"

"Why not? I mean she ain't my type, but I can see why Will liked her. She had a good figure before the baby."

"But she never hushes, and she's white."

"Uh-huh. But guess Brother Will overlooked those little facts."

Amelia shook her head. "You know, he's the one member of this family who claims to be a Keetoowah, and they preach against marrying whites. I just don't understand how they ever got together in the first place."

"Well, what I heard from his best friend, Saul Fox, is Penelope kinda trapped Will. She caught him behind the schoolhouse one night when him and his friends was at a pie supper. Kinda threw herself at him, and of course, Will didn't resist. After that they started slippin' around, meetin' in the woods, and the next thing we heard, they was gettin' married."

"Well, I just hope I don't have to see her a lot."

"They pretty much keep to theirselves ever since Pa gave them all that land and helped them build their own place." John went on to tell Amelia that in exchange for his help in the running of the family farm, their father had deeded Will an extra two hundred acres of the dark, rich Oklahoma bottomland, to add to his own allotment.

In a time when the rest of the country was reeling from hard times, Sam Clay prospered. He had inherited around four hundred acres from his father and received over six hundred acres of allotment land for himself and his children. On this acreage, he had an apple and a peach orchard, one hundred head of cattle, thirty hogs, a large flock of chickens, six horses, and crops of corn, tomatoes, beans, squash, peas, okra, turnips, radishes, cucumbers, cabbages, and potatoes. In addition, sharecroppers lived and worked on the land he wasn't farming. With the exceptions of flour, sugar, and coffee, his family raised everything they could eat, and they ate well.

Many of his white neighbors, without the benefit of allotted land, did not fare so well. With little land, and sometimes no access to a stream of water, a bare living was eked out. Many of the area's citizens, both white and Cherokee, turned to liquor as a means of forgetting their misery.

Even so, Sam didn't appear content, and neither were other Cherokees in their community. Amelia noticed that the elders of the Eagle, Wild Cat, Nofire, Hummingbird, Fourkiller, Vann, Comingdeer, Christie, and other Cherokee families made frequent visits to their house. She brought them coffee as they sat on their big front porch and talked to her father. Even though she had forgotten most of her mother tongue, she saw their grim faces and could understand enough Cherokee to know they were angry about something. After they left, she asked John what they had been talking about.

"They don't like it because Cherokee Nation no longer has any authority since we are considered to be ruled by the State of Oklahoma now. You know Oklahoma became a state in 1907?"

"Yes, they told us that at the Mission. But our teachers assured us statehood was a great improvement over Cherokee rule."

John smirked. "Well, what did you expect them to say? The matron and all the teachers were white, weren't they?"

Amelia remembered Sarah being assigned to teach the young girls. "Yes, all except one, but she would probably agree with the whites. So, are the Cherokees angry with the whites?"

"Oh, they've been mad at the whites for a long time. Some of them have even defied them and their rules, like Redbird Smith. He's been teachin' the doctrine of the Keetoowahs for many years. Accordin' to him, Cherokees should live the way they did in the old land. They shouldn't have nothin' to do with the whites and their laws, and they sure shouldn't have signed-up with the Dawes Commission or accepted allotments. Redbird and some of his followers were jailed for their beliefs, but they didn't stay long. Even Cherokees, who don't totally agree with the Keetoowahs, say we ruled ourselves better as a territory than the whites are rulin' as a state. I don't think our people are too mad at some of the whites who live around here. They've lived with us so long that we all know each other, and Cherokees and whites have intermarried. Our people consider white families like the McGinnis family and the Stones to be our friends."

Amelia understood why John differentiated between the white families. Josh Stone, the proprietor of a community general store near Clear Creek in the Jubilee community, treated all his customers, Cherokee and white, the same, with courtesy and fairness. Since most families didn't want to make an all-day wagon trip to either Aiden or Tahlequah, they were willing to pay higher prices at the Stones' store. Joshua Stone, with the help of his wife, Martha, and his five children, made a good living out of their little store.

All the Stone children were quite talkative, and one of the girls, Susan, managed to draw the reticent Amelia out of her shell a little. Amelia liked all the Stones, except for the sharp-tongued Martha, Josh's tall, snobbish, mean-spirited wife.

Sam encouraged Amelia to go home with the Stones when they asked her, because he insisted she needed socializing. He had shared his worry with John. "Something's not right about Amelia since she came back from that school. She won't even answer me when I speak to her in Cherokee, so all our conversations are carried on in English."

Of course, John promptly told Amelia what their father had said about her.

"I don't speak Cherokee because the school made me forget it. I almost got beaten to death once when I forget and spoke Cherokee. As for not being the same, how would Pa know I have changed? He only came to see me half a dozen times in nine years."

John's eyes watered as he placed his hand on Amelia's back. "I'm sorry, sis. I never knew your life was so hard."

Brushing his hand away, Amelia bent to her task at hand, peeling potatoes. "That's all right, John. It's all in the past, and I hardly think about it anymore."

At first, Amelia was hesitant about going to another girl's home, and for the first few months after she came home, she politely offered excuses for not accepting Susan's invitations. But one afternoon, after surprising herself by giggling with Susan at the store, she finally agreed to spend the night at the Stones' home.

THAT NIGHT AFTER they closed the store and had eaten a hearty supper, his children begged Joshua to play his banjo while they jigged. Dancing of any kind was completely foreign to Amelia since her teachers had condemned dancing as sinful. She was surprised to discover jigging was easy and fun once she got over her initial shyness.

Frank, the oldest of the Stone children, laughed and clapped. "Look at that little gal go! Pa, get your fiddle out, and we'll show her how to square dance."

With shining eyes, Amelia accepted and spent the rest of the evening cavorting with the dancing Stones. As she danced, she noticed that the youngest of the Stone boys, Michael, kept staring, which confused her.

When it was time to go upstairs to bed, Amelia looked around Susan's room, which she shared with her younger sister, Jenny. Like the rest of the Stone house, it was neat but simply furnished with heavy oak furniture. After settling in bed with Susan and Jenny, she asked Susan why Michael kept staring at her. Susan giggled and rolled her eyes. "Why, Amelia, don't you know that Michael's stuck on you? Frank and Ned tease him about you all the time."

"You are surely mistaken. Why would your brother have romantic notions about me?"

"Oh, Amelia, sometimes you are so funny with your proper talk and mission ways! That school might have educated you, but they sure didn't teach you common sense. Michael thinks you're pretty, Milly, and you are."

"I know now you're just trying to be nice. You're pretty, not me. You're slender and fair, but I'm dark as mud from working in the fields, my nose looks like a squashed turnip, and besides, I'm short and a bit stout."

"All I know is Michael likes the way you look, and I think you've got the prettiest eyes and hair I ever saw. And if stout means you actually have a bosom, then I wish I was stout. Now, good night. I'm tired from all that dancin'."

Amelia closed her eyes to sleep, but she kept seeing Michael Stone's twinkling blue eyes as they watched her flitting about the room earlier that night.

AMELIA LOVED HER brother, John, who resembled her stocky, usually good-natured father, except for his dark auburn hair. But she avoided going around her tall, stern, brother, William, and his white wife, Penelope. Penelope barely nodded when she met Amelia at church or in town. At the breakfast table one morning, Amelia asked John, "Am I right about this or not? The only time Penelope comes around is when she wants something."

John nodded his agreement. "She acts like she thinks she married beneath her. Personally, I would just as soon not to ever see Will as to have to put up with Penelope."

Sam paused from eating his biscuits and gravy long enough to admonish his children. "Don't talk about your brother's wife that way. Remember, she's still family."

John winked at Amelia and buttered another biscuit.

AMELIA'S SIXTEENTH BIRTHDAY came and went without anyone taking notice of it, so the next day she treated herself. John came in from working in the fields and grinned when he saw her creation. "What's the occasion? That's the first cake I seen in a coon's age."

Sam sat down at the table, saw the cake, and scowled. "Where did you get the stuff to make a black cake?"

"From the Stones' store."

"It couldn't have been cheap. We don't have money to throw away on nonsense like ingredients for fancy cakes."

"I bought it out of my egg money as a present for myself. You may have forgotten yesterday was my birthday, but I haven't."

Sam dropped his eyes. "I'm sorry, Milly. Me and the boys quit payin' attention to birthdays long ago. Let me give you a present."

Sam reached for his strongbox, opened it, and took out three silver dollars. "Buy yourself something pretty to wear."

Amelia popped the money into her apron pocket. "Thanks, Pa. I will put this to good use."

After consuming two large helpings of venison, gravy, green beans and new potatoes, fresh tomatoes, and hot cornbread, Sam stared at the chocolate cake. John, who had tasted chocolate cake twice before at church socials, noticed his father's hesitation. "Go ahead, Pa. It's real good."

Once he had taken his first bite, Sam smacked his lips. "This is even better than oatmeal cake. I could eat one of these every day."

After washing, drying, and putting away the dishes, Amelia joined her father and brother on the front porch. Sam contentedly smoked his pipe and stared at the stars. "Milly, did I ever tell you the story of how a spirit dog created the Milky Way?"

"Yes, Pa, but it was a long time ago. Remember to tell it in English, so I can understand."

"It loses a lot when you tell it in English." He fell silent and continued to smoke and rock in his old wooden rocking chair while he contemplated the stars.

He abruptly stopped rocking and removed his pipe. "I guess I might try. This is what Granny Bluebird told me when I was just a boy. Once there was this old couple who depended on their supply of corn meal to carry them through the winter. One evening the old woman went to where they stored their cornmeal in baskets, and it was nearly all gone! She ran crying to her husband. He grabbed a big stick and ran out the back door.

"He heard something gobbling up the corn, and there, by the wellhouse, was a gigantic spirit dog. When he started whipping it, the dog howled and flew up into the night sky, heading to his home in the north, howling as he went. As he ran and howled, the cornmeal fell out of his mouth, leaving behind a white trail. This became what the Cherokees call, 'Where the dog ran.' White people call it the Milky Way."

John yawned and stretched. "Good story, Pa. Haven't heard that one in a long time. Well, I don't know about you two, but a working man's got to get his rest. Goodnight. Oh, and happy birthday, sis."

"Thanks, John."

Finishing his pipe, Sam knocked the ashes out, and stood. "What did you think, Milly?"

Amelia hid her smile behind her hand. "I enjoyed it."

Sam grinned. "Well, that's good. My old eyes are closin' by theirselves. Good night and happy birthday, Milly. I been wonderin'. Exactly how old are you?"

"Sixteen."

"I thought so. See you in the mornin'."

AMELIA WAITED UNTIL her father had gone in and she could hear him snoring. Standing by her bed, she pulled off two patchwork quilts and a soft goose down pillow. Pa would call her silly, but she was sleeping under the stars tonight.

Settling herself on a comfortable pallet, she looked up again at the shimmering stars. There were thousands of them tonight, and they looked so close. Unconsciously, Amelia stood up and reached out her hand to touch one and laughed at her own foolishness. What was there about stars that fascinated her so? They seemed like living beings a person could talk to, so she did.

"Do you see me, star, like I see you? Do you know who I am? Do you know what is going to happen to me?"

She scolded herself. "Why ask a star? You know what is going to happen to you. You're going to stay right where you are, taking care of your pa until he dies unless you get married. But who would want to marry you?"

She rocked back on her heels and smiled at the answer she received.

AMELIA GOT UP early the next morning so that she could finish her heavy chores before the sun got high. Besides the usual cooking and cleaning chores, she must wash and hang out all her family's clothes, as well as hoe the garden. Amelia sighed as she hung another pair of Sam's wet, heavy overalls on the wire clothesline. At least tomorrow was Sunday, a day of worship, rest, and socializing.

Later, Amelia soaked her aching muscles in the tin bathtub during her weekly Saturday night bath, considering her outfit for church the next day. Susan had given her some pink gingham material that never sold at the store which her thrifty mother ordered her to use. "But it's the wrong color for me, Milly. Pink just makes me look too pink, but with your coloring, it should look real nice."

For a week now, Amelia had been sewing by the light of the coal oil lamp at night. After she finished her bath, she would put the dress on for the first time. She had bought a piece of pink satin ribbon with her birthday money. She was going to tie that in her hair.

Most of the time she didn't care how she looked, and her father constantly scolded her. "Amelia, get that rag off your head and put on a pretty dress. How are you ever goin' to catch a husband, lookin' like that?"

Amelia always fussed back at him. "Who wants to catch a cranky old man who would boss me around? I already have two bosses in my life, and that's two too many."

Finishing her bath, she tried the dress on in front of her dresser mirror. Bringing her long, thick, ebony hair back from her face and tying it back with the pink ribbon, she marveled at the effect. Susan was right. This pink color did something for her appearance the drab colors she usually wore had never done. Amelia examined herself closely in the mirror. No one would call her beautiful, but her tawny skin glowed with good health and youth, her glossy black hair gleamed, her dark eyes shone with intelligence, and her body was softly rounded in a womanly fashion. It was true. Time changes things, and in Amelia's case, for the better. She couldn't sleep that night because her restless mind kept living the day to come. Finally, she turned to a true remedy for sleeplessness which Sarah had taught her. She frowned when she thought of Sarah, but she prayed anyway. "Father, forgive my failings, bless my family and friends and keep them safe. Please give me rest for my body, soul, and mind." As always, it worked, and she fell into a deep sleep.

THE NEXT MORNING, Sam grinned broadly when he saw Amelia in her new finery. "That's the way a young lady ought to look."

Even John remarked, "What happened to that little brown mouse that was my sister? I don't know this woman!"

Amelia playfully punched his muscular arm and said, "Now, do you know me?"

"Ow! I know you, all right. Lord, you hit hard for a girl!"

THEY WERE AMONG the last to arrive at the small community church, and Amelia's heart fluttered with excitement. Now, everyone would see her new dress. She followed her father into church, smiling and waving to those who spoke to her, and relishing their looks of surprise and approval. They sat down directly across from the Stone pew, and each member of the family spoke to her, except Martha. Michael's blue eyes twinkled in delight, but Martha's stern face registered cold disapproval. She leaned over and whispered something to Susan.

Susan left during Sunday School to work with the children, but Amelia grabbed her elbow as she came back up the aisle during the short interval between Sunday School and the preaching service. "Come sit by me, Susan. I got to ask you something."

"All right. I guess Ma won't care."

"Did you get in trouble with your ma over giving me the material?"

"Oh, you know Ma. She has to be mad about somethin' all the time. Besides, it's worth it to see you lookin' so pretty. Hush, now, the singing's started."

This was Amelia's favorite part of church, the singing. Always before she had held back, not wanting to show off her trained alto voice, but today she didn't feel like holding back anything. As she put her heart into "Shall We Gather at the River," people around her stopped singing and stared at her.

Smiling broadly, Susan complimented her. "Why, Milly, I never knew you had such a good voice! You should sing specials."

"Oh, no, I would be too embarrassed to do that. I just like to sing."

It seemed the preacher also liked to preach because the last altar call wasn't given until well past the noon hour. "Brothers and sisters, I know, this morning, some of you aren't right with God. If you should die tonight, you would go to a Devil's Hell. Please come forward and give your heart to Jesus."

For the first time in her life, Amelia felt something tugging at her, urging her forward, but she resisted. Susan nudged her. "You ought to go forward, Milly. I did last year, and it sure helped me."

"Not today, Susan, but I'll think about it. I pray every night, but I've never gone to the front of a church before."

After the service closed, the congregation mingled, shaking hands and visiting. Michael came back to where the Stone family stood and held Amelia's hand long after he had shaken it. "You sure look pretty today, Milly. You ought to wear that dress more often."

Martha elbowed him aside. "Not until she pays for it, boy. Mister Clay, the material she made that dress from belongs to us, and I think you owe us for it."

"Of course, Missus Stone, how much do I owe you?" Sam pulled out his leather pouch and began to pour out some coins.

Even though he was at least two inches shorter than his wife, Josh Stone's outrage made him look taller. "Martha, I won't have you acting this way in church! Susan told me the material was a present from her to Amelia, and my family don't ask money for what has been given. Come on, now, it's late, and I want my dinner. Sorry, Sam, you gotta overlook Martha sometimes."

"Overlook, indeed!" Martha turned red and flounced away down the aisle.

As they drove home, Sam pointed to a small white building. "You know, I believe we need to start goin' to that new Methodist Church over there. I'm more of a Methodist than a Baptist anyway, and that Baptist preacher preaches way too long. Besides, I don't like that Martha Stone."

John snorted. "Who *does* like her? She's a mean old biddy."

"John's right, Pa. You shouldn't let Martha Stone keep you from going to church."

Sam waved to two boys who were riding their horses to Jubilee.

"See there? That's the Woolard brothers. Their family is Methodist, and they already went to church and ate dinner while we are still travelin'. Martha Stone ain't the main reason I want to change churches."

AUTUMN WAS FLASHY and short-lived, the winter following fast and hard. Amelia only saw the Stones a few times before the winter set in, but she and Susan made good use of those times to have heart-to-heart talks. The week before Christmas, before the deep snows came, Susan invited Amelia to her house for a Christmas Eve party. Amelia buzzed through the next few days, preparing for and looking forward to the party.

She even talked Sam and John into going after some grumbling on Sam's part about "fool parties." He finally agreed when he studied the clouds. "Looks like snow so I better go in case there's trouble."

THEY ARRIVED BY horse and buggy, with several extra blankets Sam insisted on taking. Amelia wore a red taffeta dress of her mother's which she had altered slightly. Although he said nothing, she noticed tears in her father's eyes when he saw her in the dress.

John held out his arm and said, "Come on, fancy lady, your carriage is waiting."

Susan and Jenny met them at the door and took their heavy coats. The house, decorated with holly branches and smelling of cedar from a freshly cut Christmas tree, was completely packed. Amelia immediately scanned the room for a quiet corner in which to hide.

Michael spotted her, grabbing her shoulders and whisking her under the mistletoe for a quick kiss. Amelia's face blazed, but she was glad to see that no one seemed to see them. Too many others were doing the same. Noticing his attention was momentarily diverted, she pulled away from Michael and located Susan.

After a bountiful dinner of stuffed turkey, chicken and dumplings, baked ham, and several kinds of sides and pies, the company gathered around Susan, playing the piano in the parlor, for a time of caroling. Amelia and Sam were asked to sing "Silent Night." After Amelia sang the first verse, her father sang the second verse in Cherokee. After he finished, he leaned over and whispered, "Let's do the last one together. You start."

Amelia couldn't help but smile when she heard how beautifully they harmonized.

Their performance was met with thunderous hand clapping. Josh chuckled at her surprised look. "You didn't know your pa was a singer, did you? Why, when him and your ma sung specials at church, you could hear a pin drop! They was that good."

Bits and pieces of nursery rhymes sung in Cherokee reverberated through her mind. After hearing her father's rich baritone, she understood why music was second nature to her.

Too quickly, the wonderful night was over. Everyone had welcomed them, except for Martha Stone, and even she wore a smile on her face all night. As they were leaving, Susan pressed a small box into Amelia's hand.

"Susan, I feel terrible. I didn't think to get you anything."

"Don't be silly, girl. It's not much, and besides you've already given me a gift by being my best friend. Merry Christmas!"

Amelia gave her a quick hug. "Merry Christmas, Susan. Thank you!"

As they drove away, Sam fretted and muttered. "We better get home in a hurry. It's spittin' snow."

AS WAS USUALLY the case in weather matters, he was correct, and only by driving the horses hard, did they make it home before the first flakes covered the grass and road. It snowed all night and the next day and continued to rain or snow for most of the following two months. They were snowbound. Sam complained as he shoveled the snow and ice off their front porch. "Never, in all my life, have I saw a winter like this."

IN EARLY MARCH, even though the air was cool, the crocus and the daffodils had sprung up. Finally convincing her father winter was over, Amelia received permission to walk to the Stone store and pick up a few necessities. When she walked through the door, she saw only a haggard, unshaven Joshua Stone.

He spoke before she had time to say hello. "Milly, I'm so glad you're here. They're all down with some kind of bad flu, except for me and Michael, and he could sure use help in takin' care of them. No women or local folks have been in because of the bad winter to ask. Can you help us?"

"Of course, Mister Stone. But first, could you send word to my pa, so he won't be worried?"

"Sure. Michael will be glad to be away from sick folks for a while, at least long enough to get Sam word."

THREE DAYS LATER, Martha's jade green eyes popped open. She looked over at the adjoining bed where Susan and Jenny lay. Martha grabbed the silver bell, which Josh had provided, and voiced a prayer. "Lord, please let Josh hear me!"

Before she could ring it, Amelia placed a cool washcloth on her forehead and offered Martha a drink of water from a tin cup. "Take it slow and easy, Mrs. Stone. You're still very sick."

Martha took a small sip and croaked out a question. "Where's Josh?"

"At the store. He asked me to help Michael take care of all of you."

"That's nonsense. A man should be able close a store down for a few days to care for his family."

"Missus Stone, you've been ill for two weeks."

"Two weeks! That's impossible! Send Michael to me."

A few minutes later, Michael appeared at the bedroom door. "Michael, have I really been sick for two weeks?"

"Yes, Ma."

"Why wasn't Missus Ellins sent for? She doesn't just deliver babies, you know. She's good at taking care of sick folks, too."

"Missus Ellins has been here, but with half the families in the community sick with the flu, she can't stay at any one house very long. She gave Pa some medicine to bring the fever down and told him to get somebody to nurse you."

"How are the boys?"

"Doin' fine. Milly let 'em up yesterday."

"How long has Jenny been sick?"

"About a week, but Milly says her case is the lightest, and she won't be sick long."

"And Susan?"

Michael hesitated, looking to Amelia for guidance. She nodded.

"Well, Ma, she's not doin' so good. Pa sent for Dr. Jamison to look at her."

"Doctor Jamison, why, he's twenty miles away! Help me up, and I'll see about my girl." Martha tried to rise, falling back on her pillow in defeat.

"You're still too weak, Missus Stone. Let me feed you a little soup, and you'll feel stronger." Amelia thrust a pewter teaspoon toward Martha's mouth.

Martha slapped the spoon away. "I don't want any soup. I want to see Susan!"

"She's unconscious, Missus Stone. Wait until she wakes up, and you can talk to her."

But Susan Stone never woke up, and, by the time Dr. Jamison arrived, Amelia knew her friend was dead.

When she had gone to check on her that afternoon, she touched Susan's hand and felt its iciness. She pulled back the quilts and felt Susan's chest, neck, and feet. No warmth. No pulse. She thanked God

Jenny and Martha were sound asleep when Amelia moved the child to her mother's bed. She closed her friend's eyes, folding her hands across her breast, and pulling the sheet over her body.

As she left the room, she met Michael. "What's wrong?"

"Susan's gone."

LEAVING OUT THE back door, Amelia sought a place to be alone in her grief. She found a dark, quiet place in the woods where she could cry for Susan Stone. Arising from her soul and issuing through her throat, the low keening startled her. But after a moment, she gave herself over to deep mourning. Martha Stone had lost a child, but she had other children. Amelia had lost her one and only friend.

When all her tears and cries were spent, Amelia arose from the ground, dried her eyes with her apron, and went back to help the family. Only those who looked closely could tell she had been weeping, and she vowed no one would see her cry.

WHEN SHE GOT back, Michael and Josh were restraining the hysterical Martha. Josh looked at her with tears in his eyes. "Milly, please go tell the preacher and his wife. They'll do what's necessary."

A few minutes later, Amelia knocked at the parsonage door and delivered the bad news to Mrs. McGinnis. "Susan Stone is dead, and the family wants you and the preacher to come to their house."

"Not Susan! Dear Lord, what will Martha do? Come inside, girl, while I get the mister."

As they were leaving to go to the store, Mrs. McGinnis turned to Amelia. "Milly, would you mind goin' by to tell the Hawks and the Sanders? Mrs. Hawk and Mrs. Sanders can help me lay the body out."

Amelia welcomed the errands. She felt uncomfortable around the grieving Stones. After she completed the errands, she walked home.

Even though she was quite a distance from home, and the sun was going down, she wasn't afraid. She had never feared the dark, and she knew every inch of the woods she walked.

IT WAS PAST bedtime when she arrived home, the family hounds barking a friendly greeting when they caught her scent.

Her father was standing on the front porch, holding a lantern. "Who's there?"

"It's me, Pa, Amelia."

Sam shone the lantern on the path to the front porch. "What are you doin' walkin' home at this hour?"

He held the light up to Amelia's face. "Who died?"

"Susan."

He closed his eyes and sighed. "That's too bad. She was a sweet girl and a pretty one."

AFTER AN ALMOST sleepless night, Amelia awoke to the crowing of their old red rooster. Opening her window, she got a lungful of the fresh spring air. Not a cloud in the sky. It was going to be a perfect spring day. Today she would cook food to take to the grieving family. Tomorrow she would help bury her best friend. When dressing, Amelia accidentally pulled out Susan's Christmas gift when she opened her dresser drawer.

As she held the fine gold locket up to the sunlight that was filling her room, she read again the inscription on the back. "To Amelia, my best friend. Merry Christmas! Susan."

Although she had known Susan for less than two years, it seemed like they had been friends forever. Her eyes spilled tears, but she wiped them roughly away. She had too much to do to have time to cry. Maybe later.

The rest of the morning she filled with a multitude of household chores, as well as a new one, cooking for the Stones. She cooked venison stew in the heavy black pot all day. By evening it was done, along with cornbread and a warm peach cobbler. After feeding her men the stew, she drove the buggy over to take the abundant remains to the Stones.

MOST OF THE community had come to express their condolences and bring food. Mrs. Sanders replied to Amelia's question about the welfare of Martha by saying, "Martha is prostrate with grief. I don't know what the funeral will do to her. Poor soul."

The rest of the family sat as though frozen. Little Jenny cried when she saw the locket Amelia was wearing. "Sister got that for you, didn't she? I remember when she had pa order it. She got me a fancy doll. I'm going to miss her so bad."

Amelia patted the disconsolate child's head, awkwardly. She didn't know how to comfort anyone.

She was relieved when Michael came to her side. "Come here, sis. Come and have some pie. Amelia brought your favorite, peach cobbler."

All the sad-eyed people made Amelia nervous, and she didn't stay long. As she was leaving, Michael followed her out and squeezed her hand. "Thanks for coming, Amelia, and for everything you've done for us."

Amelia only smiled. She couldn't trust herself to speak without crying, but she sobbed all the way home.

THE FUNERAL THE next day was a nightmare. The little Baptist church was packed with family, friends, and acquaintances of the Stones. Many wept openly, but none so much as Martha. Worst of all was what happened at the Jubilee Cemetery. As the pallbearers lowered the coffin into the ground, Martha leaped on top of it, keening. It took her sons and several other men to pry her loose, and she swooned into a dead faint. Some of the ladies placed their shawls on the ground for Martha to lie on.

When it was Amelia's turn to throw a clod of dirt on the coffin, she threw a bouquet of early spring flowers because Susan loved them. Amelia sighed and wished for the funeral to be over so she could begin the process of forgetting.

III
A NEW START
FOR AMELIA

FOR THE NEXT few weeks, Amelia performed her chores as if in a dream, her senses numb. John and Sam tried to get her mind off her mourning, but she didn't respond until one May morning when Sam whistled as he walked to the kitchen for breakfast. "Got some good news, Milly."

Placing the heavy platter of sausage and bacon in the center of the kitchen table, she turned to face her father. "And what would that be?"

"We're goin' to a hog fry and stomp dance tomorrow."

She snorted. "That doesn't sound like good news to me. I'm staying home."

Sam raised his voice. "Not this time you aren't. It would be an insult to the Cherokee families if my daughter refuses to come. We used to go to stomp dances all the time, before you were born, and even when you were a baby. John still goes sometimes. They could use your help with the cookin', and it's about time you learned about your people."

She knew by the look in Sam's eyes he wouldn't take no for an answer, so she just grumbled under her breath. As soon as the breakfast dishes were washed and put away, she poured a large quantity of pinto beans in a large cast iron pot and covered them with water to soak. After picking several yellow squashes from the garden, she gathered ingredients to make dough for fried apple pies. She would do her baking in the morning and fry up the squash so everything would be warm and tasty.

The pies, as always, turned out plump and golden, and she had to threaten John to stay out of them. "Delicious! Nobody makes pies like you, Milly."

She swatted his hands away. "Well, no one will ever know if you gobble them all up."

"All right! All right! Just makin' sure they was fit to eat."

Sam, who was holding a bundle behind his back, frowned when he saw she had put on one of her drab everyday dresses. "No, Amelia, you won't be wearin' that worn-out old dress. Wear your mother's red taffeta." He handed her the bundle. "Here's the black dancin' shawl she used to wear to all the stomp dances with that fancy red dress. You're goin' to need the shawl when the dancin' starts."

She opened her mouth to protest but shut it when he handed her the exquisite, handmade shawl. When she thought about her mother's own hands fashioning the garment, she knew she wanted it. "I'll wear it, Pa, but I won't dance. I don't know how."

"Oh, you can dance. You just don't know it yet."

ARRIVING AT THE stomp grounds a few hours later, Amelia was amazed to see how many people were there, many that she didn't know. She had always been away at school when stomp dances were held, so she knew almost nothing about the traditions that pertained to Cherokee customs. She resolved to observe and listen to everything.

She returned the greeting of *Si-yo* but merely smiled and nodded when the trio of designated cooks continued the conversation in Cherokee. She did have a general idea what they were talking about but looked around for a translator.

Sam walked over. "My girl forgot her own tongue at the white school. You'll have to talk English to her if you want her to talk back."

One round, jovial, elderly woman laughed and changed to English. "We'll talk any way she wants. It's been so long since we seen Mary's girl. Can you cook?"

"Yes, I can cook. I've brought some beans, fried squash, corn bread, and fried pies." She set her dishes down on the long wooden table.

"Fried pies, ay?" Another cook stole a peak at her covered basket. "Mary was always good at them, too. Come on, girl, and we'll show you how to cook a hog."

Despite her earlier misgivings, Amelia enjoyed her day at the hog fry. Everyone was so friendly, and they laughed all the time. Even though the little brown children were into everything and seemed always underfoot, no one raised their voices or showed anger. One little girl accidentally tripped, while she was chasing another girl, and landed in her lap. She giggled, looked up into Amelia's eyes, and said something to her in Cherokee.

An older girl pulled her from Amelia's lap and apologized. "My little sister doesn't watch where she's goin'. She's sorry she fell on you."

"That's all right. What's her name?"

"Her English name is Emma, but we all call her *u-s-di* because she's the baby of our family."

"*Si-yo, u-s-di.*"

The little girl ducked her head, but after her sister poked her, she spoke up. "*Si-yo.*" Looking at her sister for permission, she saw her nod, and ran away.

Her older sister remained by her side. "By the way, my name is Oma Littledeer. What's your name?"

"Amelia Clay."

"Oh, John's sister. It is nice to meet you."

"Yes, I'm John's sister. I'm glad to make your acquaintance." Although she tried to be discreet, Amelia had never seen so many handsome Indian men in her life, and she couldn't help staring. In appearance, they all dressed much like white men, some wearing their dark hair longer, either tied back or loose upon their shoulders, and their flashing ebony eyes seeming to glitter with mischief, danger, or both.

Once, one of the most handsome of the young men pulled back his glistening hair, which fell to his waist, and tied it back with a thick leather band. He looked up to catch Amelia staring at him. Smiling warmly at her, he gave a little wave of his hand.

One of his friends said something in Cherokee to him, and they all laughed.

Amelia's cheeks burned, and she turned to leave in shame, but Oma stopped her. "They're teasing Lakota about flirting with the prettiest girl here. Come with me, and I will introduce you. He is my cousin."

"Not now, but tell me about him. Why does he have such long hair?"

"Haven't you ever heard of the Nighthawks?"

Seeing her puzzled expression, the young woman explained. "The Nighthawks are a group of Cherokees who still practice the old customs. They say they will never accept white man ways."

"Oh, like the Keetoowahs. My brother, Will, used to be one."

"Not exactly, but many of the Keetoowahs are Nighthawks. I remember your brother, Will. He used to come to our stomp dances before he got married."

Smiling broadly, the handsome young man walked up to where they were standing. "Oma, who is your friend?"

Oma poked him in the arm. "Her name is Amelia Clay. Now, I'll leave you two to get acquainted."

Rubbing his arm, the man grinned at Amelia. "My cousin shows her love in strange ways! Hello, Amelia Clay. My name is Lakota Littledeer, and I am glad to meet you. I am so glad to meet you that I will even tell you so in English."

She returned the smile. "Well, hello, Lakota. Nice to meet you."

"I know your brother, John. He has told me all about you."

"Oh, no, if John has told you about me, then you probably don't think much of me!"

"He only said good things about his little sister. It's time for the men to eat but look for me tonight at the dance."

After the men finished eating, the women and children ate while the older men played horseshoes and the younger men, stick ball. Amelia watched and cheered with the other women as the two teams played a long rough game, grimacing when a young man was carried from the field with a broken arm. The next minute she hid her smile behind her hand when Lakota's team won, but she mostly sat and listened to the other women laugh and joke as the men made their way to a nearby creek to wash up before the ceremonies.

After dusk fell, the elders moved to the front. Comingdeer, the chief dancer and the oldest man, stood in front of the fire and spoke to the crowd. "From time to time, I feel it is good to remind our people of who we are and where we came from."

Oma, who was sitting beside Amelia, repeated his speech in English.

Amelia knew her family's history, but she listened intently as he spoke of some things she had never heard of. He began describing the way things were in the old land before the white man came. He went on speaking about how the whites, with their lust for land and gold, had driven them from their beloved homes. He ended his speech saying, "We brought part of our homeland with us. This fire is the eternal fire, which was brought from our land and which we took with us on the Trail Where We Cried. Soon we will dance the dance of our fathers and our grandfathers around their own fire. Let us begin."

At first, she sat watching as the others joined the circle and moved agilely around the flames. Lakota came and took her hand, "Come on, pretty girl. We have some turtle shells for you to wear."

Lakota turned his head as Oma quickly raised Amelia's skirts and tied a pair of leather leggings, covered with turtle shells, filled with river pebbles, on Amelia's calves.

Her face burned. "Lakota, I can't wear these. They aren't mine."

"They are my sister's, and she can't wear them because she's expecting. It's forbidden for women in her condition to wear the shells. She said you could wear them."

He led a nervous Amelia out to the dancers' circle. It wasn't long until she knew her father was right. The dancing was second nature.

She soon became intoxicated by the heart-pounding rhythm of the drums and the tinkling sound of the shaking shells. She fell in love with the graceful image of herself as the girl who moved as if one with the music, and the handsome man who danced near her.

She caught a glimpse of her father, intently watching her. He was smiling and talking in Cherokee to some of the other men who were not dancing. Once, he pointed toward her with his chin, and Amelia wondered if he was talking about her but decided she didn't care if he was. He looked happy for the first time in a long time, and she surprised herself by feeling the same way.

Sometime during the dance, she noticed that her father and John had joined the circle.

Time meant nothing to Amelia. Only the dancing existed.

She was surprised when Comingdeer announced, "Time for a rest." She could have danced on for hours.

LAKOTA GRABBED HER hand and drew her into the woods. "While the old ones rest, we will talk. I want to know all about you, Amelia Clay."

"My life is boring. I would rather talk about you."

"Me? I'm a simple Cherokee man who likes to talk to pretty girls. Or would you rather do something better than talking?"

She shivered as he drew her down beside him on a tree stump and put his arm around her shoulders.

"Are you cold, Amelia? Let me warm you up."

When he squeezed her shoulders, she remembered her mission upbringing and pushed him away. "No, I'm fine. I thought we were going to talk."

She liked Lakota's low, rumbling chuckle. "All right, let's talk. First of all, why haven't I seen you before? Where have you been?"

"At the Cherokee Girls Mission School."

"That explains why you speak so properly. Did you like it there?"

"Of course not, who could? How about you? Your English is perfect."

"Thank you for saying so. I attended the Male Seminary at Tahlequah when I was younger, but my father asked me to come home two years ago."

"Why did he do that?"

"My family are all Nighthawks. We believe in living in the traditional Cherokee way. Others of my family frowned on my father allowing me to stay at the Seminary as long as I did. My father said I must be allowed to see what it was like before I could appreciate being a Cherokee."

"And do you appreciate being a Cherokee?"

He shrugged his shoulders. "It is what I am. But enough about me, tell me more about yourself."

She told Lakota things she had never told anyone, all about the good times and the bad times she had experienced at the school. The only thing she left out was her frightening encounter with Thomas Jennings, and somehow, she felt he sensed that.

Lakota reached over and touched her hand. "Thank you for opening your heart to me. Now I know you. Come on, it is almost time to go back to the dancing."

As he took her hand to help her up from the boulder, Lakota drew her into his arms and brushed his lips against her hair. "I would like to teach you not to be afraid, sweet one. Will you let me?"

She nodded her assent as Lakota bent down to kiss her gently but passionately on her trembling lips. She was suddenly filled with strange feelings, feelings of warmth and desire. To her astonishment, she found herself returning the kiss with equal fervor.

John's laugh startled her.

"So, here you are, little sister. Pa sent me to look for you."

Quickly pulling away, she gave a feeble farewell wave to Lakota, meekly following John back to the campground.

Seemingly unflustered, Lakota asked, "Are you leaving, John?"

"Don't know. That depends on Pa."

"Let me walk back with you, so I can speak to him."

Sam had gathered Amelia's pans and dishes together and was sitting in the wagon when they arrived at the campground.

Lakota introduced himself. "*Si-yo,* I am Lakota Littledeer. Pleased to meet you."

Sam accepted the extended hand and shook it. "Good to meet you. I'm Sam Clay. Lakota, that's Sioux, isn't it?"

"Yes. It is said that my father's grandfather was Sioux, and I appear to look like him."

"I know your father, but is his wife your mother?"

"No, sir. My mother is dead. Her Cherokee name was Laughing Deer, though."

"That's what I thought. Are you of the Deer clan?"

"Yes, sir."

"My children's mother was Mary Elk. You belong to the same clan."

Lakota's face assumed a pained expression, and he closed his eyes for a minute. When he opened them, he stared at Amelia. "Little cousin, I am happy and sad to meet you."

"Pa, you never said we were related to anybody named Littledeer."

"Sorry, but the subject of the clans never came up. You are related to this young man on your mother's side. All Cherokees are of their mother's clan, and anyone in the same clan as you is your relative."

"Exactly how were our mothers related?"

"Well, that gets complicated, but near as I can figure, your great, great grandmothers were cousins."

"That means we are hardly related at all."

Lakota spoke softly, "Amelia, it doesn't matter. We are still of the same clan and are cousins. To love anyone in the same clan is forbidden."

"But why?"

"Our ancestors made this law a long time ago. As a Nighthawk, I have taken an oath to obey all Cherokee laws."

"It doesn't make sense. We couldn't be more than what, fourth or fifth cousins?"

"Perhaps, but we are related by clan law, and that is what matters. Goodbye. I hope to see you again sometime."

Sam shook Lakota's hand. "Goodbye, Lakota. It's good to see that some Cherokees still live like Cherokees."

As they drove away, she spoke up. "Well, I think the whole concept of clans is confusing and obsolete."

"Nevertheless, it is still the law, daughter, and as Cherokees, we must obey it."

She was glad the night was dark, so they could not see her tears.

She ignored John's clumsy attempts to cheer her up. "Come on, sis. You'll probably meet somebody else when we go back to the next stomp dance."

"No, I won't, because I'm not going to another stomp dance."

It would be many years before she did.

BEFORE SHE WENT to bed, Amelia took out a book of poetry her father had given her for Christmas. She sobbed when she read the lines, "For of all sad words of tongue or pen, the saddest are these, it might have been."

THAT SUMMER JOSH Stone asked Amelia to work in the store, which she did all that year and most of the next. She was glad he asked because it helped to take her mind off Lakota, but she still couldn't help but look up whenever a young Indian man came into the store.

Michael's quick eye caught this, and he surprised her one day by saying, "Are you looking for anyone in particular, Amelia?"

"What? Oh, of course not!" She got very busy again, wiping the counter and putting away merchandise.

Being at the store everyday exposed Amelia to different social groups in the community. The Stone store was as much a social gathering place as the church and the school. One group in particular amused her. This was the group of older men who whiled away the day by playing checkers, chewing tobacco, whittling, and telling tall tales. Most of them were polite to her, and some of their stories were quite interesting. By listening to their talk, she learned a great deal about the history of the community and the history of the families that lived there. She learned who was honest, who was questionable, who was poor, and who barely made a living. No one had a lot, but no one admitted his own family was poor. One day she overheard one man inviting another man to his house.

"Why don't you and the missus come over to the house for supper tonight?"

"That's right kindly. What you havin'?"

"What else? Beans and taters."

"That's what you had last time we come over."

"Oh, no, you're all wrong. Last time you come over, we had taters and beans."

One of Amelia's favorites was Anderson McKindle. He was younger and taller than most of the men, with broad shoulders and long arms. Anderson was full of wild tales and funny jokes, and there was never a man among them who was more generous. His one fault was a strong taste for liquor, which he satisfied like most folks in the community, with home brew. As his excuse for heavy drinking, he offered the pain of his stump of a leg. He had lost his leg during the Battle of San Juan Hill and wore a wooden leg, which he often took off, when he said it pained him.

She got a first-hand account of Anderson's war story one cloudy spring morning. Arriving at work that day, she was surprised to find that Anderson was the only one sitting on the front porch. "Hello, Anderson, where is everybody?"

"Probably scared of a little bad weather."

"Really? What bad weather?"

"Well, there's some that might say that one or two of them clouds look like they might carry a storm. And, as you know, storms ain't good this time of year."

She surveyed the morning sky. "Think we might get a tornado?"

"Nah, just a little wind and hard rain. Think we better go inside, though, before we get soaked."

Josh was rearranging the shelves when they got inside. "Mornin', Anderson. Amelia, you can finish stockin' while I work on my paperwork. Dark as it's gettin', we probably won't have many customers today. Anderson, let Amelia know if you need anything. I'm going to the back for a while."

"All right. Believe I'll have me a soda pop and some peanuts."

"What kind do you want?"

"I like a ginger ale with my peanuts. Hand me the scoop, and I'll get my own nuts. Would you like one?"

"Not right now, but thanks for the offer. All right. Here you go."

She took out a cold pop from the refrigerated soda case, opened it, and handed it to Anderson. "That will be seven cents."

"That's a bit high, aint it? I just paid a nickel for it last week."

"Josh said we got to charge two cents for the peanuts now. He said everybody was eating too many because they knew they were free when you bought a pop."

"Well, I guess I can't fault him for tryin' to make a profit. Do you mind if I talk to you while you're workin'?"

"No, not at all."

Anderson moved a little three-legged stool over to the area where Amelia was working

"On stormy days like today, my poor old leg gets to painin' me something awful." He grimaced as he rubbed his hand over his upper thigh. He stopped and stared at her as if trying to recall a memory. "Amelia, did I ever tell you the story about meetin' some of your kinfolks during the war?"

"No, I never knew about that. Who did you meet?"

"His last name was Wolf, and he was from North Carolina, but when he was a boy, his folks told him he had kin near Tahlequah."

"He may have been related through my great-grandfather. I believe his name was Grey Wolf."

"That's a good name. Say, why is it some of the Cherokees have white names now?"

"Probably because they married into white families, like my family did once."

"Maybe so. Anyway, we was livin' in Arkansas at the time, and I took a notion to ride my horse down to Texas to visit a cousin who lived there. When I got there, he talked me into volunteerin' to fight in a war that was brewin' in Cuba. I was just a fool kid and didn't know what I was doin'. Turned out my cousin wasn't fit to serve, but they took me all right. I was so lonesome, and most of the fellers in my company laughed at the way I talk. Called me, 'the bumpkin.'"

"Why didn't you just tell your commander?"

"Things don't work that way in the army. Them fellers would have all jumped on me and beat me to death. Well, anyway, on with the story. One day the captain brought in somebody new, Emmett Wolf. He was a quiet man, short and stocky, and very dark complected. His darkness got the attention of the bully boys."

"What happened?"

"Soon as the captain left, they started callin' him names. He ignored them at first, but when one of them shoved him, he must have decided that enough was enough. He turned around and kicked his attacker's feet out from under him, and then he started beatin' the livin' hell out of him!" Anderson clapped his hand over his mouth. "Oh, sorry, Miss Amelia, that slipped out. The big man didn't know what hit him. I can still see him layin' there with that stupid look on his face! Well, everybody left him alone then, but they still wasn't talkin' to him. I looked close at him and saw he looked like a lot of Cherokee friends I had, so I struck up a conversation. Best I remember it went like this. I noticed him walkin' around by himself one day, and I hollered at him. 'Hey there, are you a Cherokee?'

"That got his interest, and he said, 'Yeah, but how did you know?'

"'Well, sir, I'm from Jubilee close to Tahlequah, Oklahoma, and I know a lot of Cherokees. I sure admire what you did the other day.'

"'What's that?'

"'When you put that bully boy in his place.'

"'He deserved it.'

"'Yes, sir, he did, and it gave me an idee.'

"'What's that?'

"'Thought me and you might be friends. I bet I know some of your kin. They's Wolfs that live in Jubilee.'

"Then we started talkin', and he told me about bein' from North Carolina but bein' kin to people who live close to Tahlequah, and I told him what I knew. I told him I heard tell of a man named Grey Wolf who lived in Jubilee before the Civil War. And you know what he said?"

"What?"

"'Grey Wolf's granny was my great, great, great aunt!'"

"So, we are kin. I wish I could meet him."

"I would dearly love to see him again, too, but I seriously doubt if I ever will. Anyway, back to the story. We become the best of friends and fought side by side, all over Cuba. He saved my neck more times than I can count, and I even saved his, a time or two." Anderson paused. "Then I lost my leg, and things changed."

She stopped sorting cans and looked directly at Anderson. "Do you want to talk about it?"

"Sure. I don't mind. It happened somewhere in Cuba. I forget the name of the town, and I can't pronounce it, anyways. Me, Wolf, and the other men was out patrolin'. Nobody had told us there was enemy soldiers in the area. The big bully boy was the first one killed. The captain checked on him to see if he was dead and said, 'Fall back!' We all scrambled to retreat. I took a bullet when I was runnin' away. Wolf drug me out of there somehow. If it hadn't been for him, I wouldn't be here today."

"Whatever happened to Wolf?"

"I don't really know. I passed out from all the blood I lost. When I come to, I was in a field hospital, and they was gettin' ready to load me up and take me to a hospital in Florida. My leg got infected, so they had to cut it off, but they was kind to me. After I recovered, they sent me back to Arkansas, and they fitted me with this fake leg. Wish't I could have thanked Wolf for savin' my life all them times."

"Maybe you will see him someday."

"Not likely. I don't even know if he's alive. Could I have another scoop of them nuts?"

"Sure, but don't tell Josh."

"Not a word. Here comes the rain."

Heavy rain and small hail began pelting the tin roof of the store. "Told you it weren't a tornado, just a little thunderstorm."

AMELIA KNEW ALMOST all the McKindles, including Anderson's father and uncles, had served time in the state penitentiary for moonshining. Even though everyone knew Anderson and some of his kin still made it, so far, they had been lucky. One day their luck changed.

About mid-morning a pair of hard-looking men ran up to the store. They called out, "Quick, Anderson, we need your help!" and started to pull him out the door with them.

"Hold on, fellers. Let me put my leg on. I took it off because it was hurtin' so bad."

Amelia and a crowd of spectators were watching the proceedings. She asked, "Who are those men?"

"Why, girl, that's Ben Black and Clyde Bishop. They're part of the gang that robbed the Ft. Smith bank th' other day."

"What do they need with Anderson?"

"They probably want to borry his car to git away from the law. Heard they had to leave their car in the woods a ways back."

Anderson was still struggling with his leg, and one of the men spoke up. "Fellers, we need somebody to drive for us. We ain't got time to wait on Anderson to get his leg on."

Anderson's youngest brother, Benton McKindle, volunteered. "I'll be glad to help you if Anderson will give me his keys."

"Much obliged, Bent. Come on, then."

As they ran out the front door, Anderson laughed and called to Benton. "Give them lawmen a run for their money, Bent. There ain't no way they can catch you once you get past the bridge. Wish't I could go with you."

While the men in the store began to laugh and compare stories of their run-ins with the sheriff and his deputies, Amelia noticed that Tom Guilder slipped away from the crowd. She watched as he asked Josh if he could use the newest addition to the Stone store, the first telephone in that part of the country.

"Sure, help yourself. Do you know how to use it?"

Tom nodded and quickly turned away from Amelia and Josh to make his call.

The next day, Anderson came storming in with the bad news. "Some yeller dog tipped the sheriff off about Ben and Clyde. They got them right before they got to the bridge."

"Are they all dead?" asked Josh.

"No, just poor Bent. The others got away, but the law's lookin' for 'em, all over the woods and hollers. And poor Bent left a wife and two young'uns!" Anderson took a long draught from his jug. "And my car shot all to pieces. Anybody know anything about who turned 'em in?" He fixed his wild blue eyes on each man's face, in turn.

No one said anything, and Amelia kept her thoughts to herself.

"Who's not here today?" Anderson grabbed Josh's forearm.

"Hold on there, Anderson. Let me take a look around before you squeeze my arm off."

"Hurry up then!" Anderson took his large, freckled hand off the smaller man's arm and glared at him.

"Well, Grandpa Smith ain't here, but he's sick in bed, so you can't suspicion him. Moe Glory is home with his wife cause she's havin' a baby. Oh, and Tom ain't here." By the time he finished speaking, he was almost whispering.

Later Amelia asked herself why she spoke up. Maybe it was Anderson's icy eyes, wild with grief. Maybe it was because Tom

Guilder had always acted like she was invisible. Or maybe it was because she knew too well about betrayal and loss. Whatever the reason, she heard herself saying, "Tom made a telephone call yesterday when you were talking to the other men."

"Did he make it before or after Bent left?"

"After."

"That's all I need to know. Thank you, Milly." Anderson stalked from the store, swinging his jug with each step.

Amelia didn't dwell on what happened in the store that day. If she thought of it at all, it was to hope that Anderson didn't go on a binge and get hurt again. The friendly giant of a man wouldn't really hurt Tom. Perhaps just scare him a little.

The next morning when she walked into the store, she encountered a grim Michael. "Milly, last night Tom Guilder's house and barn burnt down.

"Was anybody hurt?"

"No, but they lost everything they had, even their animals. They'll probably be movin' pretty soon."

"Won't the men build them another house and barn like they did for the Nofires?"

"I don't think Anderson would allow that."

"So, Anderson is behind it all?"

"I didn't say that, and you better not say it either when the sheriff comes around."

"Don't worry. I won't say anything."

"Good."

Anderson came in later that day, laughing and joking with the other men as usual. Suddenly, Moe Glory let out a war whoop as he ran inside the store. "Better get yourself out the back door, Anderson. I just seen the law down the road a piece, and he's comin' with his siren a blarin'. You can take my car. I parked it around back for you."

"Much obliged, Moe. Meet me at the mill tonight, and you'll get your car back." For once, Anderson had on his leg, and he scrambled out the back door.

THE NEXT DAY, Anderson didn't come to the store. After getting used to seeing him every day, Amelia realized she missed talking to him. After a week had gone by, she decided to ask Josh. "Where is Anderson these days, Josh?"

"You know I was just wonderin' that same thing, Milly. Wonder where that ornery cuss is keepin' hisself? Could be he got worried about trouble with the sheriff over Tom Guilder, and he's on the scout now. Sheriff looked pretty riled-up when he was in here, questionin' everybody the other day."

Martha snorted and hissed. "Why you two want to worry about that low-life is a mystery to me! What is all that noise I hear outside? Go see, girl, and come back and tell us what is goin' on?"

As she ran to the front porch, Amelia spotted a large carriage rolling down the road, stirring up dust and the ire of all the area dogs. She ran back in to give her report. "It's a big fancy carriage, being drawn by six fine black horses. The dogs are making a racket, barking at it."

Martha grabbed her arm. "Well, go back out there, and see if it's comin' here. If it stops, you need to be there to ask those fine folks to come in. Such people are usually free with their money, and we could use the trade."

Reluctantly, she straightened her hair and sat on a bench on the front porch to wait. She didn't like meeting new people, but she had to obey her boss.

A few minutes later, the carriage pulled up to the front of the store, as the driver yelled, "Whoa!" She stared as the wind-burned, middle-aged driver opened the carriage door and handed out a lady, swathed head to toe in black silk, and helped an elderly, dark-skinned cowboy, sporting a gray Stetson, down from their transport.

Remembering her orders and her manners, she walked over to where they stood. "Hello, folks. Would you like to come into the store to get a drink of cold water and rest a bit?"

The lady removed the long black scarf that covered her head and face. *"Gracias.* That is very kind of you."

The old cowboy took off his hat and stared intently at her face. "Is that you, Little Milly?"

Startled, she hesitated before answering him. "My name is Amelia Clay, and I work here at the Stones' General Store."

He chuckled and grabbed her hand. "Don't be afraid, Milly! I'm your uncle, Junebug Clay, and this is my wife, Maria. We come to see your pa, but I will take you up on that offer of something cold to drink."

After a flurry of buying fine tobacco, fresh coffee, and an assortment of sodas and candy, her uncle winked at a delighted Martha. "I don't suppose you'll mind if I take my niece along with me when I visit her pa?"

Martha put on her friendliest face. "Of course! We can manage without her for one afternoon." The face stayed friendly, but Amelia could hear the warning in her tone. "See you bright and early in the morning, Amelia."

"All right. Thank you, Missus Stone."

"My pleasure."

AMELIA SAW TEARS glistening in her father's eyes when he caught sight of his brother. "I never thought to see you again, June."

Junebug grabbed him in a fierce bear hug. "I'm sorry I waited so long to come and see you."

Sam stepped back and grinned. "Well, the road runs two ways. I should have gone to see you long ago. But that's in the past. Come in, come in! Milly, fix them somethin' to eat, all right?"

Maria patted Amelia's arm. "Don't worry yourself. I packed a big basket of tortillas and other food. We stopped and ate several times on our way and won't be hungry for some time."

Amelia said nothing but hurried into the kitchen to make some coffee and cut a chocolate cake for serving. In a few minutes, they were all gathered around the table, eating and reminiscing. She had heard stories about Junebug all her life, but they were more real when he told them himself. "Did you really kill an outlaw when you were just a boy?"

June stopped in mid-laugh and turned solemn eyes toward Amelia. "Yes, I did. Only man I ever killed, though I will admit there has been some that wisht they was dead, after I got through with them. I shot him because I had to save my mama. He would have killed her, and no tellin' how many others, if I hadn't ended his wickedness. I've had a lot of regrets in my life but killin' that bad man ain't one of them."

In the next minute, he had them all laughing when he told how Old Sam got the best of the shrewd horse trader, Katie Christie. "Katie didn't want to sell the paint she had bought for her son, but Pa wouldn't take no for an answer. I found the horse, and my heart was set on havin' him. I had him blanket and halter broke in record time, and he came when I called him. That still wasn't enough for Katie. I had to ride him in front of her eyes. Imagine that! A kid ridin' a horse that had never been rode or even broke."

John was staring at his uncle, completely caught up in the story. "How did you do it?"

"Granny Bluebird told me that a Seminole horse might respond to a Seminole word. I whispered *e-ree,* which means mine, and he let me ride him. Pa bought the horse for a hundred and twenty-five dollars and some meals for Katie and her family. You see Katie didn't like to cook, and she insisted on getting food thrown into the deal."

After they all laughed, Sam chimed in. "That horse, Warrior, was one of the best horses I ever knew. June gave him to me when he went off to Texas, and I rode him for several years until he died of old age."

Since her father seldom talked about her mother, Amelia had some questions for Junebug. "Why did my mother die so young? No one has ever told me what she died from. And why didn't you ever come back to see us after she died?"

Her father and uncle exchanged glances. Sam said, "Go ahead and tell her," and stared down into his coffee cup.

June sighed and paused before resuming his speech. "Best I remember, measles was goin' through the community. Will, John, and Mother Star all got them. The boys recovered, but Ma passed away. Mary was expectin' and wore herself out takin' care of everybody. Maria came and tried to help her, and your pa hired a nurse. The baby died, and Mary just never recovered her strength."

"As for comin' back to see you, I was scared and superstitious. I got the stupid idea that this place was cursed because sadness and death just seemed to linger here. When I was in Texas with my family, I could live and laugh and forget about the pain you were goin' through. Of course, it didn't help that as soon as I got back to the ranch, Mr. Goodnight sent me on a hunt lookin' for some cattle rustlers which had been plaguin' him. That kind of kept me busy for quite a while. But excuses aside, I know I acted selfish, and I'm sorry I let you down."

June leaned over and patted Amelia's cheek, and she could see the deep creases that crisscrossed his brown, weathered skin. Up close she could see that, even though his hair remained black, he was thinner and older than he first appeared to be. "Will you forgive me, Milly?"

"Of course, Uncle June. Truth to tell, I probably wouldn't have been here if you had come to visit. Pa put me in the Cherokee Girls School when I was six."

Maria murmured something in Spanish. June leaned closer to her and cupped his ear. "What's that, Maria?"

"I said, if I had known Sam was going to put her in a mission school, I would have taken Amelia to our house to live." She glared at Sam. "And if you had answered my letters, maybe that is just what would have happened!"

Sam closed his eyes for a minute, shook his head, and turned toward Amelia. "It's me who should be askin' your forgiveness, Milly. I was in such a dark place that I didn't want any reminders of your mother's death. I didn't read them letters until seven years had passed. By that time, you seemed happy at the school, and I saw no reason to move you to Texas."

Junebug stood up. "Well now, that's water under the bridge, and there ain't no reason we should keep grousin' about it. Come on, Sam, show me around the old place. It looks like it's growed considerable."

"That it has. I added about six hundred acres by allotment. We can ride over to Will's place, and you can meet his wife and children. John, go out and saddle us up some horses. Do you girls want to go?"

Maria shook her head. "No, I am glad to get away from horses. It's good to sit in a house for a spell. Maybe you can invite them all over here for a meal, and I can meet Will's family then."

Although it pained her to think of sharing a meal with Penelope, Amelia just smiled and said, "That would be fine. I will stay here at the house with Maria and get things together for supper."

SHE HAD TO bite her tongue when Penelope dominated the conversation at supper the next day. According to Penelope, their oldest daughter, Rosemary, was the smartest child in her school, and her younger sister, Virginia, was the prettiest. If Maria said anything good about one of her sons, Penelope had to top it by repeating a supposed compliment which someone had paid one of her daughters. When Maria praised Amelia's chocolate cake, Penelope offered to give Maria her recipe for coconut cake, which the preacher said was the best cake he had ever eaten. When June or Maria directed a question at Will, Penelope would interrupt his answer with her own view on the matter. Finally, Maria stopped talking and just rolled her eyes at every statement Penelope made.

As soon as Will and his family rode away, June let out a great sigh. "Thank goodness they left! That woman about wore me out with all her talkin'!"

Even Sam, who usually defended Penelope, had to laugh.

Junebug, Maria, and their hired man, Felix, stayed for four weeks before June started talking about going home. "Guess we better start off early in the morning if we want to beat the fall rains." They were seated at the kitchen table, enjoying some fried peach pies and homemade ice cream. "Amelia, you are a good hand at these pies. Taste just like your mother's pies." He stood up and motioned for Maria to stand beside him.

"Come on, Maria. Let's get this over with."

As Maria walked around the long wooden table, Amelia noticed the worry in her dark eyes. She placed a trembling hand on June's shoulder.

"Besides gettin' to see all of you, there's another reason we made this trip." Junebug looked away as if to regain his composure. He sighed and looked at Sam. "Sam, you're the only brother that I ever had, and I had to tell you."

"Tell me what, June?"

"I'm dyin'. Doc says I got cancer. Cancer in my gut, and I don't have long to live. I wanted to see you one more time before I go."

Sam let out a strangled cry and drew his brother close to his chest. John and Maria joined the brothers, patting and consoling them. Amelia left the table.

SHE WENT OUTSIDE and walked to one of her favorite places in the woods where she sobbed and cried for several minutes. After she got her cry out, she dried her eyes, and went back to the house. By this time, everyone was behaving normally, and she cleared off the table and prepared to wash the dishes.

Maria grabbed a washcloth. "I'll wash, and you dry since you know where everything goes."

"You don't have to help wash dishes. You're company."

"No, like I told you before, I'm family. We can wash dishes and talk. You know I miss having someone to do this with. June and I had three ornery boys, and I always wanted a daughter."

"And I always wanted a mother."

"Ah, it's too bad that neither of us got what we wanted. But you know what?" Maria stopped washing dishes and smiled at Amelia.

"What?"

"The wife of our oldest son is expecting, and I may soon be holding a granddaughter."

"Will Uncle June get to see her?"

"We hope so. But you know what else?"

"What?"

"Someday, you will be a mother yourself."

Amelia smiled into Maria's happy, dark eyes. "I hope so."

When Junebug said his last goodbyes the next morning, Amelia hugged him and said, "I'm sorry, Uncle June."

"Don't be sorry, Milly. Who would have thought a poor little Indian boy would have had such a grand life?"

AS THEY WAVED and drove away, Sam said, "I would like to go see him in Texas before he dies, but it's a long trip."

John patted him on the back. "I'll take you whenever you say."

"Let me think on it."

THE FIRST FRIDAY in October, Amelia saw Anderson, all dressed up in fresh pressed clothes and clean shaven, standing beside his new shiny Ford, which he had parked in front of the store. "Hello, Miss Amelia, could I have a word with you?"

Amelia, who had been sweeping off the front porch, put down her broom, "Well, hello, Anderson. Good to see you again. Come sit down on the bench and talk to me."

Anderson awkwardly climbed up the steps to the bench. He sat down beside her and grinned sheepishly. "I want to ask you something."

"What's that?"

He hesitated for a few minutes and then blurted out his news. "I'm gettin' married on Sunday at the Baptist Church, and I want to ask you to come to the weddin'."

She raised her thick dark eyebrows in surprise. "Really? Sure, I wouldn't miss it. Who's the lucky bride?"

"Ella O'Dell."

"That's odd. I thought I knew everyone who lives around here. Where does Ella live?"

"She lives over at Cane Hill."

"Oh, she's from Arkansas. How did you meet her?"

"I have a brother named Jack who lives over there. Last summer and early fall I stayed over at his house for a spell to help him bale hay. I may be slow and clumsy with this leg, but I'm strong as an ox. Anyway, while I was staying there, he invited me to go to church with him and his family. That's where I met Ella. Prettiest girl there and the sweetest! I didn't think she would have nothin' to do with me because of the leg and her bein' considerably younger than me. I was sure surprised when she turned out to be friendly. We been keepin' company ever since. Last month I asked her to marry me. She wanted to, but her family was dead set against it. Her ma said she could do better than a one-legged good-for-nothin'."

"Her pa asked me, 'How are you going to support our daughter?'"

"What did you say to convince them?"

"Well, I just showed her pa my government check I get every month for my leg. Know what he said?"

"What?"

"'That's more than most workin' men get around here in half a year. You have my blessin' as long as you get married in church. That way it will last.'"

"How about her mother?"

"She still hates me, but I hope to change her mind in time. Ella's from a big family, so she will likely have a lot of people there. Jack and his family will stand up for me, but that's about all. My sister, Lucinda, never comes here no more, and my other family has all moved off. Then, of course, Bent's not with us anymore, and his family has gone back to live with his wife's folks. I would sure appreciate it if you would be there as my friend."

"Anderson, you have plenty of friends besides me."

"True, but none of them go to church on Sunday, mainly because they's hung over from Saturday night."

"Are you going to do the same as them?"

Anderson shook his head. "Nah, not anymore. I'm goin' to be too busy learnin' how to be a good family man."

"Well, I am glad to hear that. What time is the wedding? "

"Two o'clock in the afternoon."

"I will be there."

After Anderson left, she finished sweeping and went back inside.

Josh had been looking out the store window at Amelia and Anderson. He peered at her over his glasses that had almost slipped off his nose. "Who was you talkin' to, Milly?"

"Anderson McKindle."

Josh frowned in seeming disbelief. "Are you sure you was talkin' to Anderson?"

"Yes."

"It sure didn't look like Anderson."

"You probably didn't recognize him because he looked so nice. He's getting married, and he invited me to his wedding."

"Well, imagine that! Anderson McKindle gettin' married! Who's he marryin'?"

"Ella O'Dell from Cane Hill."

"I didn't think it was a local girl. Never knew of him to court anyone from around here."

"I wonder why. He's a handsome man when he cleans up, and he always has money."

"Them McKindles don't have a good reputation. Anderson's father and uncles all served time in the penitentiary for moonshinin', and he came mighty close to it himself when he was young. Bein' in the war and losin' a leg seemed to settle him down some. At least he mostly quit moonshinin' except when he's helpin' out his kin. When he got back from the war, most all the women his age was already married, and parents kept the young ones away from him."

"Well, I hope Anderson and his bride will be happy." She wanted to get the new couple a nice wedding gift, so she started looking around the store.

Josh, sitting on a stool at the counter working on his accounts, stared up at her. "Are you looking for anything in particular?"

"Oh, just something that would make a pretty wedding gift. Did I see some new merchandise in the back room?"

"You sure did. I just haven't gotten around to unpackin' it. Why don't you do it, and you can look at all of the pretties while you unpack them."

Putting aside his book work, Josh grabbed a piece of scrap paper and did some quick figuring. "Say, I tell you what I'll do. I'll give you a ten percent discount if you spend at least three dollars on somethin', fifteen percent on five dollars or more."

"That sounds fair enough. I'll see what I can find."

She was holding up a Blue Willow platter and sugar bowl, trying to decide which to buy when someone grabbed her waist and shouted, "Boo!"

"Michael, you almost made me drop these, and if I had, I would have made you pay for them!"

"Sorry, just couldn't resist huggin' my favorite girl."

She slapped his hands away. "Who says I'm your girl?"

"I do! Now, how about a kiss?"

"Michael, I'm working!"

"Pa won't mind if you take a break."

"Not now, Michael!" She gave him a hard shove, and Michael knocked a box over, which fell with a loud thud.

"Now see what you done, Amelia! All because you wouldn't give me a little kiss."

Hearing the noise, Josh came in and pulled Michael away. "Quit botherin' my help, Mike. If you need something to do, you can help me load feed for my customers."

"All right! All right! See you later, darlin'."

She smiled after Michael and his father left. Michael was good-looking, and it was nice to be admired. She set the Blue Willow sugar bowl aside for purchase and continued to unpack the merchandise. The fancy sugar bowl would cost her all her week's pay, six dollars, but she had some money saved up, and she wanted to show Ella's mother that Anderson had real friends in Jubilee.

THE NEXT MORNING, Amelia got up extra early and started cutting up vegetables for stew. John popped a piece of carrot into his mouth. "Ain't you goin' to church with us?"

"Not today. I've been invited to a wedding at the Baptist Church this afternoon."

"You could go to both."

"Yes, I could, if I knew for sure that we would get out of church by noon, but since we changed preachers, most of the time lately, it is almost one. That wouldn't give me enough time to come back here, fix you and Pa some dinner, walk to the wedding, and get there before two. I am going to stay home, fix a meal, that I can leave on the stove if you and Pa are late getting home from church, and leave for the wedding at one."

"You never said who's gettin' married."

"Anderson McKindle."

"Really? So, why are you goin' to that scoundrel's weddin'?"

"He's a friend of mine, and he invited me."

"Hard to picture you bein' a friend of Anderson's."

"Why is that?"

"Well, he's not exactly the kind of man a lady like you would associate with."

She slapped his hand away as he reached for another piece of carrot. "Quit eating up all the vegetables! John, just because I'm a lady doesn't mean I can't like who I want to like."

"Sister Amelia, I am going to accompany you to that weddin' whether you want me to or not. A lady has got to think about her reputation. Besides, Pa would make me take you anyway if he got wind of what you are goin' to do."

She let out an exasperated sigh. "Oh, for goodness sake! All right. You can go with me but wear your best suit and polish those old scuffed up boots you always wear."

"With pleasure, my lady. What's for dinner?"

"Stew and cornbread. It's easy to keep warm."

"What, no cake?"

"I worked all day yesterday, and I was too tired last night to do much. Be thankful that you get a warm meal at all."

Sam grumbled a bit when Amelia told him about her Sunday plans, but he agreed with John that she needed an escort. "Take the buggy, John. I can ride Scout. It'll do us both good. Don't remember the last time him and me went for a gallop."

"Thanks, Pa."

"You're welcome. Just don't make a habit of not attendin' your own church. We're Methodists again, not Baptists. Congratulate Anderson and his new wife for me."

"I don't plan on doing this again, and I will congratulate them for you."

"All right, then."

THE BRIDE'S SIDE of the church was packed, just like Anderson said it would be. On the groom's side, only two pews were occupied. Amelia managed to arrive early so she could get a good look at the O'Dell family. It was easy to pick out Ella's mother. She was the small, red-haired, dark-eyed woman, sitting on the front pew, with her arms crossed and a big scowl on her freckled face. Anderson was going to have his work cut out for him to make his mother-in-law like him.

John saw where she was looking. "That old lady looks like she just ate some sour pickles!"

"S-h-h-h, John! Someone might hear you!"

The wedding was short and simple. Ella was dressed in a pink print dress and carried some pink peonies which matched her dress. She appeared to be just a little older than Amelia, but she carried herself with a quiet dignity. Anderson, on the other hand, was sweating profusely and had a hard time standing still. He was dressed in his only suit, the one he had worn to his brother's funeral, and he had taken time to carefully comb his hair and shave his face. He would have looked handsome if his forehead wasn't soaked in sweat. He stopped fidgeting when his bride walked down the aisle, and the love she inspired in him shone from his eyes.

After the ceremony, Amelia and John approached the beaming Anderson. "Amelia and John! Glad you could make it. This is my wife, Ella."

Ella took Amelia's hand. "I am so glad to meet you, Amelia. Anderson has told me a lot about you."

"Hope it was good. This is my brother, John."

Ella extended her hand to John, and he pressed it briefly. "Hello, Ella. Nice to meet you. Our father, Sam, sends his congratulations to you, Anderson."

"Thank him for us, would you? Sam's a good old feller."

"John, would you go get their wedding gift from the buggy?"

"You didn't have to get us a present, Amelia."

"I know I didn't, but I wanted to, so I did. Here, let me get out of the way so you can visit with the rest of your guests."

Ella's eyes shone when she untied the pink ribbon which bound the large white hat box that John handed her. She removed the tissue and brought out the delicate Blue Willow sugar bowl. "Oh, it's beautiful! Look, Ma, at what Amelia gave us!"

The sour-looking woman finally smiled. "Why that's right pretty! Blue Willow, ain't it? I used to have a few pieces of that myself, but somehow, they got broke over the years. Thank you, young woman, for givin' my daughter such a nice gift."

Anderson reached for Amelia's hand and squeezed it. "Yes, thank you, Amelia! We sure do appreciate it!"

"Just enjoy it, and if you put it on your table to sweeten your coffee and other food, maybe you will remember me and the friendship we share. Now, John and I need to get on home. Congratulations and best wishes to both of you!"

Ella looked disappointed. "Won't you stay and have some cake and coffee? My sisters made a big, fancy wedding cake, and it would make me happy if you would stay and eat with us."

John grinned. "You don't have to ask me twice. Come on, Milly. We got plenty of time. It won't be dark for at least three hours."

As Amelia and John walked over to the serving table, she heard Della O'Dell say, "Now that was a lady, and she gave you a lady's gift. She would be a good friend for you, Ella."

Amelia was sitting by Ella, chatting and getting acquainted, when she heard Ella's father clear his throat. Everyone abruptly quit chatting. "You know, I heered from men who know that some of the Cherokees over this way sell their allotments fairly cheap. I won't never be able to buy more land over in Arkansas because it's too high, but if I could get some cheap land here, then I might could get ahead considerably."

"You know, if you had listened to me and moved over here when they was givin' away them allotments, I could have claimed my Cherokee blood and got us some free land."

"Now, Della, don't bring that old tale up again. What's done, is done! It's too late now to do over, so let it drop!"

Della sighed deeply, shifted in her chair, and looked at Ella. "Well, like I told your pa, there's nothin' keepin' us in Cane Hill no more since you got married. Your brother, Arthur, is always takin' his family off to California to make some money pickin' fruit or the like. They're gone for months at a time sometimes. Bob and Marie have lived in Colorado for years. George, Emma, and their kids have put down roots in Missouri and seldom come to see us. And it's the same for Dick and Carrie. I was really surprised to see them all come in from Missouri for your weddin'. 'Course Sean disappears for months on end, and we never know when he will turn up. Looky there! He was just here a minute ago, and now he's gone agin. Esther and Wade over there already live in Jubilee, and Kate and Jed are moving here soon. Now, you'll be livin' here, too. It might be time for us to move this direction."

Amelia looked at Anderson and noticed he seemed to be listening to Zeke and Della's conversation with some consternation. His face fell when Ella said, "That would be wonderful, Ma."

"Well, we haven't decided for sure, but we're thinkin' strong on it."

Before anything more could be said, Anderson took Ella's arm. "Come on, honey. You need to introduce me to the rest of your folks before they have to leave out." He turned toward Amelia and John. "Thanks again for comin'. Don't forget to take some cake home for your pa."

John said, "We'll do that. Come on, sis. I need to feed before it gets plumb dark."

When they got out of earshot, he chuckled. "I got the feelin' that Anderson would just as soon his in-laws stay over in Cane Hill."

"I think you're right."

WHEN AMELIA AND John got home, they couldn't find their father. "That's odd. Pa usually stays close to home on Sunday. Maybe he's over at Will's. I'll ride on over and see."

"All right. I'll look around here. Maybe he took a walk."

She spotted him sitting by the branch that ran through their land. Climbing down the hill, she sat down beside him on a fallen log. "Pa, are you all right?"

"I'm fine. Just got an urge to sit by the branch for a piece and smoke my pipe. You know, around here somewhere is where my pa found June. If he hadn't of dove in and grabbed him, he would have been a goner for sure."

"I know. I had heard that story several times, but I liked it best when Uncle June told it."

"That June was always a storyteller, but we won't hear any more of his tales."

"What do you mean? We just got a letter from Aunt Maria last week, talking about how happy he is with their first granddaughter. It sounds like he's doing fine."

"He's not fine now. He's likely dead, and I broke my promise to him."

Amelia gasped. "Why would you say such a thing?"

Sam removed his pipe and turned to face her. "While you and John was gone, a screech owl came and roosted in the big oak by the front porch. I tried to scare him off, but he just kept sittin' there, making his ungodly racket. Finally, I went into the house to get a gun to shoot him, and when I come out, he was gone."

She scooted closer to her father and touched his shoulder. "You believe he was a messenger, warning you someone in our family was going to die, don't you?"

"Yes, and now it's too late for a visit."

She rose to her feet. "Now, Pa, you know that's just an old superstition. Aunt Maria said Uncle June is improving, so we aren't going to worry about him. Let's go to the house. Anderson sent some cake home for you to eat."

"Well, hope you're right. Be there in a minute."

THREE DAYS LATER, John rode to town to get some supplies. He came back with the supplies and a telegram, which had come in on Monday. With shaking hands, Sam took and read it. He handed it to Amelia.

It was from Maria, telling them Junebug had passed away suddenly on Sunday afternoon. She wiped away a tear and patted her father's arm. "You were right. I'm so sorry, Pa. Do you want to go to the funeral?"

"Nah, we can't get there in time. It's day after tomorrow. Goin' to take a walk. Maybe you can write Maria a letter while I'm gone." He left by the back door.

ON SATURDAY EVENING, Amelia agreed to watch their children while Bill and Mildred Johnson spent the evening and night at a relative's house in Tahlequah. Ab Miller, one of Amelia's favorites, came by with a rick of wood he had cut for the Johnsons. Ab was the complete opposite of the talkative Anderson. He was quiet and softspoken until he came into contact with children. Then his small dark frame took on the guise of a flamboyant actor as he told his spine-tingling tales to a young audience. They loved his stories, and seemingly, the scarier, the better.

As soon as he stepped in the door for his pay, the Johnsons' four children set upon him. "Uncle Ab, tell us a tale."

"Go along now, young 'uns. Miss Amelia don't wanna hear none of my tales."

"She won't mind. Will you, Amelia?"

"No, indeed. In fact, it sounds like a good way to pass the time."

"All right, then. Just one. Let's all set down here in front of the fireplace. Circle in here. There was onc't this old widder woman that I knowed. She lived all by herself in a little ol' house deep in the woods, acros't a little lake, far away from ev'rbody. It was awful lonesome, livin' by herself like that. She was always wishin' for some company, but nobody ever come. One night she got so lonesome, she went plum crazy and called out, 'Who's gonna sleep with me this cold winter night?'"

"Then way across the mountains she heered ..." Changing his voice to some unearthly creature's, Ab wailed, 'I will!'"

"Well, she set on her front porch, and she smoked her pipe, and she rocked a bit, and she smoked her pipe, and then she said, 'Who's gonna sleep with me this cold winter night?'"

"And somethin' gettin' in a boat and startin' acros't the lake said, 'I will!'"

"So, she smoked her pipe, and she rocked a bit, and she smoked her pipe, and then she said, 'Who's gonna sleep with me this cold winter night?'"

"And somethin' about halfway acros't the lake said, 'I will!'"

"Well, about this time, she was startin' to get skeered, so she went in her house and started gettin' ready for bed, but as she was gettin' ready, she couldn't help sayin', 'Who's gonna sleep with me this cold winter night?'"

Amelia smiled as eyes doubled in size and little bodies scooted closer to hers.

"And somethin' gettin' out of a boat said, 'I will!'"

"Now she's gettin' in her bed, and even though she bites her tongue, she still says, 'Who's gonna sleep with me this cold winter night?'"

"And somethin' walkin' through the woods says, 'I will!'"

"Now she's layin' in her bed, thinkin', tryin' her best to keep quiet, but she can't help but say, 'Who's gonna sleep with me this cold winter night?'"

"And somethin' comin' up on her porch says, 'I will!'"

"She's takin' her specs off to go to sleep, and she whispers, 'Who's gonna sleep with me this cold winter night?'"

"And somethin' says, *'Gotcha!'*"

At this, Ab grabbed Betty, the nearest child by the shoulder, and she screamed. "Oh, Lord, Ab, I about peed my pants!'"

Amelia didn't tell the children, but she felt the same way.

After she had taken Betty, Spencer, and Susie to the outhouse because they wouldn't go by themselves, Amelia sat by the fireplace, talking to Ab. He seemed very nervous to be alone with a young woman and remained silent as he chewed vigorously on a large chew of tobacco. "Ab, you really have a way with children. Why is it that you never married?"

"Now, Miss Amelia, who would ever want to marry an ugly old cuss like me?"

"Don't sell yourself short. Men like you are rare."

"I don't know 'bout that. Speaking of marryin', when are Mike and you gettin' married?"

"Who said we were getting married?"

"Why, Mike's told ever'body that you and him's gettin' married right soon."

"Really? I wish he would have asked me first."

"Now, Miss Amelia, don't get riled. Mike don't mean nothin' by it. He's just crazy mad in love with you. Don't tell him I mentioned it. Guess I better be gettin' home. It's gettin' late, and it looks like it could storm."

After walking Ab to the door, she stirred up the fire, and stepped outside to take a long look at the sky. The black clouds did look threatening. Time to put the children to bed.

She lay awake beside little Susie, pondering what Ab had told her. Did Michael really love her? If he did, why didn't he tell her? Oh, he was forever trying to catch a stolen kiss, but he seldom talked to her seriously about anything. But if he did love her, how did she feel about him? She knew she loved many things about him, his dancing blue eyes, his lilting laughter, his boyish face and physique, and his clever mind and hands. But did she love him? She didn't feel the same way as she did with Lakota, but she suspected she would never feel that way about Michael or anyone else. Little Susie had kicked off her covers, and the room was getting colder. Amelia picked up the colorful patchwork quilt from the floor and gently settled it back over Susie. She smiled as Susie murmured something about "kitty cat." Amelia dreamed of having children of her own to care for and love. She fell asleep dreaming about her future.

A few hours later, Amelia awoke to a terrifying roar that filled the whole room. Her mind played back stories she had heard about tornados. The old-timers said you always heard a roaring sound before one hit. She quickly grabbed up Susie, shook awake Betty and Spencer, who were sleeping nearby, and went to awaken the oldest boy, James, who was sleeping in a corner of the parlor. She was surprised to find him already awake and staring out the window. "Would you look at that?"

"James, get away from that window and help me get your sisters and brother to the storm cellar!"

"All right, all right! You can't blame a feller for wantin' to get a look at a real tornado. I ain't never seen one before, have you?"

"No, I haven't, but we won't see another one if you don't help me."

Leaving the house on their way to the cellar, little Susie whimpered as Amelia struggled to keep her quilt-wrapped body from being torn away by the great wind. Having ordered the children to stay close, she was glad when they obeyed, attaching themselves to her body like small leeches. Amelia heard the cows bellowing in fear, and she was relieved they were all in the barn. The family dog ran to James, crying piteously. James bent to pick him up, but the wind tore him away from his grasp. "James, we don't have time to fool with animals. Forget the dog!"

"I can't do that. Old Rags is like a member of the family. I gotta save him."

"Suit yourself then, but we're going on."

Looking like a mother hen with wings full of baby chicks, Amelia pushed against the wind to make her way to the cellar. When she finally got there, she found she couldn't open the heavy door. She squinted into the flying dust, looking for help.

"Put that dog down and help me, or we're all going to blow away!"

A sudden calmness now enveloped the yard, and again Amelia remembered a saying about "the calm before the storm."

"Now, James, before it hits!"

James reluctantly put Rags down, used all his strength to help Amelia open the door, pushed his siblings and Amelia in before him, and ran back to catch Rags, who was clawing at the ground, struggling to stand upright in the strong gale.

"Leave him, James!"

But with a Herculean effort, James threw Rags into the cellar and closed the door behind him just as the storm hit.

AMELIA AND THE children huddled in the darkness as the outside world fell into chaos. A tempest roared, and tree branches cracked and fell in the woods nearby. Chickens squawked, cows bellowed, and horses whinnied. The three younger children clung to

Amelia and cried. The furious wind banged against the cellar door, and Amelia expected it to open at any moment. The children cried harder. Taking a deep breath, Amelia recited the Lord's Prayer and all the other prayers she could remember. Gradually, as time went on, the storm diminished, and James searched for creature comforts.

"Hey, Amelia, here's the coal oil lamp and matches that Pa put here for storms. I'll light it so we can see somethin'."

Susie whimpered. "I'm hungry!"

"Oh, shut up! We've got food all around us. See all Ma's preserves."

Amelia said, "Too bad we have no way to open them."

James reached deep into his overalls. "I never go anywhere without my knife."

"You mean you sleep with your knife?"

"Of course, a man can't be too sure, can he?"

They soon enjoyed a feast of canned vegetables and apple preserves, and Amelia forgot her earlier irritation at James. Everyone felt better after they ate, and Amelia agreed when Spencer wanted to sing songs and play games. It would take their minds off what was happening outside. Amelia realized the roar had disappeared, and hard rain was pelting the cellar door. Perhaps the tornado had moved away, but she wasn't taking any chances. She spread Susie's quilt out for the exhausted children to sleep on, and she and James waited for the letup.

AFTER SOME TIME, she and James dozed off, too, and she was awakened by the sound of light rapping on the cellar door. "Amelia, are you all in there?"

"Yes, Mister Johnson, we're all safe."

"Just a minute, and I'll lift this branch off the door and let you out. Help me, Mildred."

She heard the Johnsons' grunts of exertion as they struggled to lift the heavy tree branch off the cellar door. "Hurry, Bill, I want to see the children!"

"Mildred, I'm hurryin' as fast as I can. "

A few minutes later, Amelia and the children squinted into the bright sunlight. Mildred's big, blue eyes spilled tears as she hugged each of the children and checked them for injuries. Bill lifted Spencer and the girls out of the cellar and ruffled James' hair affectionately. "Miss Amelia, I thank you for savin' my children."

"If you're going to thank me, you better thank James, too, because he helped me open the cellar door and kept us from getting too hungry."

"Yes, sir, I guess he ain't a little boy anymore."

James huffed. "Pa, I ain't been a boy for some time."

BEFORE AMELIA COULD get her things together to leave, she was startled to see John ride up on his big bay stallion. "Milly, climb on. You're needed at home!"

She scrambled up behind him. "What's this all about, John? Is something wrong with Pa?"

"Oh, no, Pa's fine. And Will is fine, too. It's his house that's not so good. It blamed near got blowed away in that tornado last night! They're going to be stayin' with us for a while until they get a new place built."

Dark thoughts churned in her head as she watched the trees blur past. She could barely tolerate sharing a meal with Penelope, much less live in the same house with her for Lord knows how long.

WHEN PENELOPE WELCOMED her with a broom and dustpan, she knew she had been right to worry. Amelia bit her tongue to keep from telling Penelope what she thought in the days that followed. Amelia was constantly being ordered about—washing dishes, peeling vegetables, doing Penelope' s finery, as well as scrubbing the rest of the family's laundry on the scrub board. Penelope saw dust where none appeared to exist to Amelia. She worked Amelia so hard at washing windows, scrubbing floors, and cleaning the cook stove one day that Amelia's arms and legs ached all night. The next morning the oldest child, Rosemary, giggled as she poured cold water on Amelia's feet. "Mama said for you to get your lazy self up."

"Lazy, I'll show you who's lazy!" Amelia raged as she struck the child again and again with a leather belt.

Hearing Rosemary wail, Penelope came into Amelia's room, which she now shared with Rosemary and her younger sister, Virginia. Incensed, she grabbed the belt out of Amelia's hand and shoved her roughly to the floor. "You, wicked creature! I ought to use this on you! Don't you ever lay a hand on a child of mine again, or I will!"

Sam stepped in to intercept Penelope's intended assault on Amelia. "Hey, now, what's going on here?"

"Granddad, she was beating Rosemary like a mad woman!"

"You've got the mad part right. I am mad, mad from having to live with *you!*"

Sam tried to calm them down. "Now, girls, we must get along. We're family."

"She's no kin of mine, and I'm not staying here if Penelope and her brats stay here another minute!"

"You don't mean that, Amelia."

"Oh, no? Watch me leave." She stuffed clothes and other belongings into a big leather suitcase.

Sam put his hand on her shoulder. "Stop this foolishness, Amelia."

She turned to see Will and John watching the scene. Will glared at her. "Let her go, Pa, if that's what she wants. "

John attempted to lighten the situation. "Come on, sis. Don't let a cat fight run you off."

But Amelia's eyes were staring straight ahead, and her mouth was set in an immovable straight line. She walked past her family like they were invisible, and she slammed the door behind her.

IV
THE
MARRIAGE

MICHAEL GRINNED BROADLY when he saw Amelia walk into the Stone store, dragging her heavy suitcase after her. His blue eyes danced. "Amelia, are you finally going to elope with me?"

His eyes widened and shone when Amelia replied, "I will if you will give Jasper Walkingstick fifty cents. I told him I would pay him that if he would give me a ride to town."

He paid Jasper and whisked Amelia away before his parents, who were in the back of the store, knew she was on the premises. They rode away in his father's spare buggy to the Justice of the Peace in Tahlequah, who was Michael's friend. They were married in a short ceremony and hastily booked a room in the local hotel. That night, her wedding night, the frightened nineteen-year-old relived her traumatic experience with Thomas Jennings. Michael was bewildered when his young bride cried and shivered at such a happy occasion. But when she wouldn't tell him why when he asked her, he said, "You're just nervous. Now try to relax. I've been waitin' for this for a long time."

He continued to repeat, "Just relax," every time he took Amelia to bed. But the tears and trembling continued for several weeks of their new marriage.

One night he slapped her. "Quit actin' like a baby!"

That time Amelia obeyed. She obeyed so well that she never showed any emotion at all in their intimate moments in the years that followed.

At the first slap, Amelia realized the marriage was a mistake, but she tried to deny it. She told herself, "At least I don't have to share a house with Penelope." But after a few days of living and working with Martha Stone, she acknowledged she had chosen the greater of two evils. Martha not only put the heavier share of housework on Amelia, she also expected her to work long hours in the store—for no pay, of course, since Amelia was now family. Even worse, she sensed Martha believed Michael married beneath him, even though she never actually said it.

As for Penelope, she and Will never rebuilt their own house but instead stayed on in Sam's house, claiming they were "looking after Pa." They took over Sam's allotment, but Amelia and John refused to sell them their allotments, even though Will offered a good price.

John built himself a small house on the most distant point of the property, but he only lived there a year or so before he left the country. She suspected the sharp-tongued Penelope had driven him away.

She tried everything she knew to coerce Michael into moving out themselves. She fixed all his favorite dishes, even though Martha said, "Amelia is making a mess out of the kitchen."

She tried to fix herself up, and with great self-control, managed not to shrink away when he touched her. In time this became easy for her—she removed herself mentally from her surroundings. But Michael ignored all her entreaties. "There's no sense in us movin' out now. Pa and Ma need us to help out, and I don't have the money to support you yet."

Amelia yearned to tell him what she said aloud when she was alone. "You could support me if you would save some money instead of throwing it away on cards and horses."

But, of course, she didn't. She soon learned Michael Stone loved nothing as much as a good card game, unless it was to watch a fast horse run. He was good with horses, and no one around could gentle a horse like Michael. But he was forever buying promising young horses and training them for future races, and their feed and supplies were costly. Of course, he said he must go to Aiden, Tahlequah, or Sallisaw every weekend to "check the competition," and she suspected he placed a few bets while he was there.

Since loving methods did not work, she tried the age-old resort of disgruntled housewives, nagging. Michael ignored her complaints at first. One evening, she said, "I would never have married you if I had known we would have to live with your parents all of our lives."

His face blazed red, he cuffed her ear, and said, "I don't want to hear another word out of you."

So, he didn't. For several weeks, she didn't speak to him in private at all and would barely grunt out an answer when he asked her something at the store or in front of his family.

Finally, Josh pointed to the mute Amelia at the dinner table and asked, "What's wrong with her?"

"Nothin', Pa. She's just mad 'cause she ain't gettin' her way."

"What does she want?"

"To move out on our own."

"Well, you can't blame the gal for that. It's just nature for a woman to want to build her own nest."

Although she remained stone-faced, Amelia secretly smiled inside. Josh was on her side.

But then sharp-tongued Martha joined in. "And how can they build a nest when they're poor as church mice? Let them get a little saved, and then they can talk about movin' out."

"I guess you're right, Mother. We had to live with Ma and Pa Stone for about three years."

"Three years, nothing! I waited on that mean-mouthed mother of yours for six years! If ever I got up my nerve to buck her, she would say, 'Watch your tongue, girl! You're fortunate that the likes of you are part of our family. Why, the Stone family sailed from England on the Mayflower, and I have it on good authority that my husband is a direct descendent of Sir Randall Stone of Folkestone,

England. You should feel honored indeed that we tolerate your impudence at all."

"And just my luck, less than a year after we moved out, she fell deathly ill. I served that proud old vixen, hand and foot, right up until the day she died, and I can't honestly say I was sorry to see her go. Amelia here doesn't know how good she has it, especially under the circumstances."

Amelia remained silent as her mind replayed what she wanted to say. *What circumstances? Do you mean because I am an Indian? If this is good, I don't know how much more of this goodness I can stand. Six years!* She had barely survived one year living with Martha, and her stomach curdled at the thought of another year. In a flash of insight, she remembered the "Jack with the proud past" that Old Annie had spoken of when she told Amelia's fortune. How odd! *Maybe I will tell Michael about that someday, if I ever talk to him again.*

This battle of wills went on for several weeks. Michael finally got her to talk to him by threatening to "beat her black and blue if she didn't start talkin'." But she only said what was necessary, not one word superfluous. Until one day, after they had been living with her in-laws for almost two years, she had a weapon, one that she knew wouldn't fail.

That night as they were preparing for bed, Amelia leaned over and kissed Michael on the cheek. "Michael, we're going to have a baby."

Michael's eyes lit up like in the old days and he fairly crowed. "Why, Milly, that's wonderful!" He grabbed her and hugged her with real affection.

Seeing the time was favorable, Amelia took the next step. "I hope your folks won't mind a crying youngster. You know how nervous your niece, Janie, makes your Ma."

"Oh, but Janie's just a spoiled brat. Ned and Theda never make her mind. Ours will be the first Stone grandson."

"How can you be so sure?"

"I just know. I always knew my first one would be a boy."

"This house is already so crowded. I don't know where we'll put a baby, and that Jenny, coughing all the time. I hope the poor baby can sleep."

At this last remark, Michael frowned slightly, and Amelia knew she had made a dent.

SHE TRIED NOT to act surprised five months later when he took her to an old two-story farmhouse he had found, six miles from the Stone store. "Man told me that his missus hated livin' so far from civilization. Can you believe any man would let his woman tell him where to live?"

Amelia agreed this was hard to believe and quickly began her task of settling-in to a new home before the baby arrived. She barely made it in time. In fact, she always wondered if her pushing herself so hard was what made the fair-haired Susan come a bit before she was expected.

Michael acted disappointed at first, because the expected son was a daughter, but he good-naturedly clapped her on the back and said, "Next time we'll have a boy." Not exactly welcome words to a woman who had just endured twenty hours of hard labor.

Amelia was delighted with little Susan and would sit for long periods of time, rocking and crooning to the chubby sweet bundle. Even with the extra work that came with an infant, she felt happier than she had for a long time. She finally had her own family and home.

Just two years later, Amelia was preparing to have another baby. This time the labor was much easier, but Michael was less understanding when dark-eyed, brown-skinned Emily was born. He frowned and said, "Another girl?"

He redoubled his efforts to, as he was fond of saying, "Get a boy," and a year and a half later, Randall Clay Stone was born. Amelia prayed she would finally get some rest

Michael seemed quite pleased with Amelia when she had Clay, and even let her call him after her family as long as he picked the first name. He didn't know that Amelia was going to see to it that everyone in the family called him Clay, which they did. "Look at those long arms and legs, and the hands and feet on that boy! Wonder where he got that size?"

Martha, who was visiting, spoke up. "From my side, of course. My father was called "Big Swede", and they say my grandfather was even taller." She patted the baby's chubby cheeks. "This one takes after my side and shows his Swedish blood."

Amelia was less happy now with three demanding babies, all less than five-years-old. It was not long before little Susan was expected to help with household chores and was switched when her efforts did not measure up to Amelia's standards.

A coffee-colored, black-haired, smallish baby boy arrived the following year. Amelia said, "This one looks like a Cherokee. I want to name him Samuel Ross."

Michael placed his thumb in the baby's palm. "Looks like another strong son. Name him whatever you want, honey."

Michael was an affectionate father but was content to allow Amelia to "take care of the kids," and rarely intervened. Although he managed a small family farm, raised beef cattle for sale, and helped Josh out at the store, he always found time to work with his horses and race his quarter horses on the weekends.

Amelia's body thickened with the continuous childbearing. On an average, she had a child every one to two years, and she was secretly happy when she miscarried twice after Ross was born. Six years lay between Ross and Mary, and she was glad to get the rest. She couldn't remember a time when there hadn't been someone crying for something. Her temper and nerves became more frayed as time went on, and she was often close to the breaking point.

BUT HAPPY DAYS were not unheard of at the Stone residence. One bright spring morning, Amelia had just finished hanging out the weekly wash when four-year-old Mary ran up to her with a message.

"Pa says he wants you to go sit on the front porch. He has something he wants to show you."

"What is your pa up to now?"

"I don't know. He just said for me to tell you that."

"All right. I'm going," Amelia reluctantly picked up her empty clothes baskets and walked to the front of the house. When she climbed up the stone steps, she was met by her eldest daughter, Susan, who handed her a glass of sweet tea.

"Pa says for you just to sit in your chair and rest for a bit. The show will start in a minute or two."

"What show?"

"You'll see."

Grinning from ear to ear, with his father's fiddle in hand, Michael lined the children up until they stood in front of Amelia. "Lady, just sit back and let your family entertain you. Susan, are you going to join us?"

"No, I'll sing from back here while I mind Zack. If I don't watch him, he will walk right off the side of the porch."

"Suit yourself. Are you ready, children?

"Yes, sir!" yelled Emily, Clay, Ross, and Mary.

Michael struck the chords of "O Susanna," to the children's accompaniment of "O, Susanna, do not cry for me...."

Amelia and Susan smiled and clapped their hands in time with the music. Amelia was surprised at how the children sang in perfect harmony. After they finished, she applauded. "That was wonderful, children! I had no idea you could sing so well."

Michael raised her right hand to his lips and kissed it. "How could they not, Milly, with a mother who can sing and dance like an angel?"

Susan giggled. "Ma, I know you can sing, but I never saw you dance."

"Oh, she is as light on her feet as a feather. Come on, Mother, show them how you can dance. Come dance with me, and Clay can play us a waltz."

He handed his old fiddle to Clay. "Just the way I showed you, son."

"Oh, Michael, I haven't danced in so long. I will just make a fool of myself."

"Lady, I won't take no for an answer." Michael pulled Amelia to her feet and took her in his arms. Clay played the waltz, and they moved as one for the first time in a long time.

As soon as Clay played the last note, Michael said, "Now, let's speed things up. Show these kids how their mother can jig. Give me the fiddle back, Clay."

For a few minutes, she was sixteen again, lost in the beat of the fast music. After the music stopped, ten-year-old Ross stood before her. "Please show me how, Ma. I want to learn to jig."

"Me, too, Ma," they all called one by one. Amelia danced with her children in a wild celebration, forgetting her anger against them and their father.

Before she knew it, an hour had flown by, and little Zack let out a wail. "Goodness, kids. Zack is hungry, and all of us will be soon. It's almost noon time. Girls, we better get some food on the table."

"All in good time, Milly. It's time to pay the fiddler first."

"What do you mean, Michael?"

"Come and give us a kiss, darlin'."

The children hooted with laughter as Michael grabbed Amelia in a fierce hug and gave her a resounding smack.

"Michael, turn me loose, so I can feed the baby."

"All right, but tell me one thing. Did you like our surprise?"

"Yes, I certainly did! Let's do it again soon."

Michael was unusually loving and attentive to Amelia for the rest of that day, night, and for several days, which was probably why she found herself pregnant yet again the next month. Her disposition turned sour and resentful again. She had hoped that Zachary was her last child. Now, she would have two in diapers at the same time—again.

ONE MORNING SHE stood at the hot cook stove, using her apron to dab at sweat dripping down her face, as she stirred a cast iron skillet of thick white gravy. Michael and the boys all sat, waiting on the girls to finish bringing the platters and bowls of hot food to the table. She noticed Clay ladling food on his plate before all the food had been served. He could be such a glutton! Something about Clay just naturally irritated her—perhaps it was his awkwardness. He was so much bigger than the rest of her other children, and he always moved more slowly. His younger, darker, and much smaller brother, Ross, could throw a rock at him or kick him and run away before Clay barely knew what had occurred. Or perhaps it was the fact that Michael clearly favored Clay above the rest of the children. Her own personal favorite was the dark, sly, mercurial Samuel Ross, who was called Ross. He reminded her of her own people, both in looks and in personality.

Later that week, Amelia was cooking breakfast again when she heard a knock at the door. "Susan, answer the door. I got my hands full."

A few minutes later, Susan came back in with John. "Ma, this man says he's your brother."

"He *is* my brother, silly goose! Hello, John, good to see you!" Amelia wiped her hands off on her apron and crossed the room to give the visitor a hug.

"It's good to see you, too, sis! Where did you get all of these kids?"

"Well, if you came back for a visit once in a while, you would know that I have been married to Michael Stone for almost sixteen years, and we have had a lot of children during that time."

"I stopped by the store and Josh told me where you and Michael live, but he didn't mention a houseful of kids. It sure is good to see you again, Milly! I wish I could say this was a social call, but it's important that we talk today."

She felt a sudden flutter of fear in the pit of her stomach, but her outer demeanor reflected calmness. "All right, John. Susan, feed the babies. The rest of you, go ahead, finish eating, and get ready for school. Susan, you can stay home today to help with the little ones."

Susan grinned. "Sure, Ma."

"Emily, Clay, Mary, and Ross quit staring and finish breakfast. This is my brother, Uncle John. You can meet him properly when you get home from school. Come in the parlor, John, so we can talk in peace. Would you like some breakfast?"

"I already ate, but I would take some coffee."

"Emily, bring your uncle a cup of coffee."

Emily hurried from the kitchen, walking slowly with a big cup of hot coffee. "Thank you, Emily. I must say, sis, you have well-behaved children."

"Oh, you came on a good day. You should see us when the older ones are fighting, and the young ones are all crying."

"Well, I'm glad I came on a good day. Now I have something serious to talk to you about. When was the last time you saw Pa?"

A sense of dread came over Amelia, and her legs turned to rubber. Seeing she was about to faint, John grabbed her arm and steadied her. "Oh, sis. I'm sorry! I should have thought about how that sounded before I said it!"

He pulled a chair out from the kitchen table and helped her sit down. "Pa is alive, and he isn't missin'. I didn't mean to upset you. Emily, please bring some water for your mother."

Emily came in quickly, carrying a glass of water, accompanied by Susan. Emily handed the water to her mother while Susan anxiously asked, "Are you all right, Ma?"

Little Mary peeped around the corner, sobbing and crying.

Amelia soon regained her composure. "I'm fine, girls. Go settle Mary down. "

She turned angry, dark eyes on John. "Don't ever do that again, John! You had me thinking the worst!"

"Please forgive me, sis. I haven't been around women in so long that I forgot how to talk to them. But could you tell me if you have seen Pa lately?"

She shook her head and blushed. "I am ashamed to say it has been several weeks since I have seen him. You know how I feel about Penelope. I still don't go to the house because of her being there, but Pa comes here now and then. He likes eating supper with us, and he loves playing with the kids. I guess we haven't really seen him since

Christmas, about four months ago. I had Abigail not long after that. Michael has talked to him at the store a time or two since then."

She looked at her brother's face and saw fatigue and fear in his eyes. "You're starting to scare me again. Now, tell me what's wrong."

"Well, he's feelin' poorly, and he wrote me a letter to come home. That's why I'm here."

The feeling of dread began to rise again. John quickly stepped to her side and took her hand. "Oh, I didn't know! It must be bad if he asked you to come home! "

She spotted Clay and Ross, standing quietly in the corner of the room. "Didn't I tell you boys to get ready for school? "

Clay looked dumbstruck, but Ross boldly said, "We was just worried about Grandpa. Is he all right?"

John went over to the boys and patted them both on the back. "Now, boys, you know your grandpa. He's tough as nails, just a little under the weather is all. Now, you better do what your ma says and get ready for school."

They kept looking at him until he shooed them with his hand. "Go on, now." He sat back down and sipped his coffee.

After the boys left the room, Amelia resumed the conversation. "You know, if he's feeling bad, you would think that Will would send me word."

Her eyes sparkled when John grinned like he did in the old days, when he was about to make a joke. "Now, you know Brother Will doesn't sneeze unless Penelope gives him permission."

She giggled and covered her mouth. "That's true, but give the Devil her due, at least she takes good care of Pa."

"Well, that's another reason he wrote me."

Her heart hammered with anger. She stood and balled her fists up. "What did that hussy do to my pa? If she hurt him, I will make her pay!"

"Easy, sis. All Pa said was they had a big fallin' out, and he wants me to move him back into my old house."

She ransacked a nearby roll top desk for something to write with.

"Wait a minute, John. As soon as I find my pen, bottle of ink, and stationery, I am going to write Pa and tell him he needs to live with us."

"Don't bother lookin'. Pa said you might want him to live with you. He said he didn't want to hurt your feelings, but he says he needs lots of quiet to get better."

She sighed. "Well, I guess I can understand that, but is your old house fit for him to live in?"

"It should be in a few days. I just got to fix it up and clean it up a little. I will go get him from Will's house, and maybe he can stay here for a little while until I get the house ready?"

"Of course. The kids will be overjoyed to see him, but I will warn them to take it easy on him."

"Sounds good. I'll go get him." John stood to leave. As he turned around to say goodbye, he noticed Amelia was staring into space like she had forgotten he was there.

Fists balled again tightly at her sides, she bit off her words. "You let me know if that Penelope gives you any trouble. If she does, I will go to her house and throttle her!"

John put out his hand in a gesture of peace. "It's all right. She's ready for him to leave. I think they had a pretty big fight."

"Well, that doesn't surprise me a bit. I don't know how he has put up with her for all these years! He should have left there a long time ago."

John opened the front door. "All right then. Don't worry about anything. See you in a few hours."

She stared at her brother's face. Once, he was always smiling and making jokes. Now, he looked worried and sad. "John, before you leave, I want to tell you something."

"What's that?"

"I have missed you, and I'm glad you're home."

"Thanks. I didn't know how much I missed you and Pa and my old place until I rode up today. It's good to be home."

He walked back to where she was standing, gave her a quick hug, and closed the door.

AFTER JOHN LEFT, Amelia called, "Emily, come here!"

"What is it, Ma?"

"We have a lot to do today, so I will need you to stay home and help Susan."

Emily's face fell. "Do I have to today?"

"Yes, you do. "

"But today is the seventh-grade class spelling bee! If I win it, I will be in the school spelling bee and maybe even the county spelling bee! Please, Ma, can't I please go to school today?"

She hissed out a warning. "Don't make me tell you twice, girl!"

Clay intervened for his favorite sister. "Ma, can I take Emily's place and stay home instead? I don't have to be at school today."

"What good would it do to keep you at home? You're a boy, and you don't know how to do housework or tend to babies."

"Ma, I help Susan and Emily sometimes. I can sweep and mop and do all sorts of stuff. Let me try, please, and if I don't do the job, I'll take a lickin'."

Amelia's heart softened when she saw Clay's love for his sister, but she sounded firm. "All right go on to school, Emily, and win your spelling bee. Clay, you can stay here, but I will have my eye on you, and you better do a good job."

Emily's plain little face looked almost pretty when she smiled at Clay. "I will, Ma. I promise."

"All right. First of all, you need to move all of your and Ross's things out of your bedroom, so you can get it ready for Grandpa Clay. He's going to stay here for a few days until he can move in with Uncle John."

"Where should I move everything?"

"Just store it in the pantry for now. We will fix you boys a pallet to sleep on in the parlor while he's here."

JOHN AND SAM came back three hours later. "Sorry, we're late, sis, but I had to stop at the town café and feed this feller."

Amelia noticed her father's hand was trembling as she took it in her own. "You could have eaten here, Pa. We always have plenty."

"I didn't want to put you to any more trouble than I am already makin' for you." Sam started coughing uncontrollably.

"Clay, bring some water for Grandpa, quick! Here, Pa, sit here in this chair and rest yourself."

Clay rushed into the room with a too-full glass, sloshing some onto the floor before he handed it to his grandfather. "Careful, Clay! You're so clumsy!"

John noticed Clay's stricken face and quickly intervened, "Don't worry about it, nephew. It's just a few drops, and I am cleanin' it up with my hanky right now."

"Don't bother yourself with it, John. The floor probably needs a good mopping anyway. Leave the glass here, Clay, and go see if Susan needs any help."

John winked at Clay and was rewarded with a grateful smile. Clay bent down and spoke to Sam. "Good to see you, Grandpa."

"Good to see you, too, Clay. You must have grown a foot since I seen you last! You're already taller than me and almost as tall as your pa." Sam's eyes darted around the room. "Where's that Ross?"

"Emily and Ross are at school, and the rest are here with me today." Her voice hardened. "Clay is supposed to be helping Susan." She waved Clay on his way.

"Are you feeling better, Pa? If you wait a few minutes, Abigail should be awake. I don't think you've seen her yet. She's just three months old."

"I'm all right, but I better not get too close to the baby. I don't want her to get this cough I have."

"How long have you had it?"

"A couple of months, but it's better than it was. Sequoyah Owl has been doctorin' me with coltsfoot, and it's helpin'. That's what Penelope was fussin' about. Said she didn't like my nasty medicine clutterin' up her kitchen. I told her it was really my kitchen, and I could have what I wanted in there. She said maybe I should just live somewhere else then. I agreed with her, so here I am for now. As soon as John gets his place fixed-up, I will be movin' in with him."

"Now, you know you and John can stay with us as long as you need to."

"Thanks, sis. I may be stayin' here tonight, and Pa will stay here until I get the house livable. I am going to ride over in a few minutes to see how bad it is. The house hasn't been lived in for over fifteen years, so it probably needs a lot of work. I'll come back tonight and give a report."

Sam got up from the chair. "I can come with you and help."

"No, Pa, it would be better if you stay here where it's warm. You don't want to get that cough stirred up again. Just stay and visit with Amelia and her kids."

"That's right. Stay here, and I will stir you up a chocolate cake."

"That sounds good. Penelope hardly ever makes anything sweet."

After John left, she asked, "Would you like to lie down and take a nap? Clay and Susan have your room ready."

"I am a little tired, so I believe I will."

Two hours later, a bouncing Emily came bursting through the door, "I won, Ma! I am the seventh-grade spelling bee champion!"

She put her finger to her lips. "S-h-h-h-h. Grandpa is asleep."

"No, I'm not," Sam came into the kitchen, licking his lips. "The smell of that black cake bakin' woke me up. Now, what's this about somebody bein' a spellin' bee champion?"

Ross spoke up. "It's Emily, Grandpa. She's the seventh-grade champion."

Sam feigned surprise. "Oh, I thought maybe it was you, Ross."

"Nah! I'm not much of a speller or a writer, but Ma says I run like a deer, just like Uncle Will when he was a boy."

"That's real good. And, Emily, you are a scholar and a good speller, just like my mother, Star, was. I think champion spellers should be rewarded. Here's a quarter you can spend at your Grandpa Josh's store."

"Thanks, Grandpa. I am going to be the school champion next."

Ross gave a shrill whistle, and everyone turned to look at him. "Good! That got your attention. To celebrate Grandpa's bein' here and Emily winnin' her spelling bee, we should all have chocolate cake with buttermilk right now."

Amelia grinned and shook her head. "Now, Ross, it needs to cool a little, but after it does, and I frost it, we can all have a piece to celebrate. Just don't let it spoil your supper."

"It sure won't spoil my supper! I could eat the whole cake!"

"Well, just because you can doesn't mean you should, Clay. Now, all of you, go clean out your lunch pails and wash your hands."

John and Michael came back in time for a supper of fresh pork chops, pinto beans, fried potatoes, turnip greens and cornbread. Chocolate cake was served to those who hadn't eaten it earlier. "Man, this is sure good, sis! I haven't had good food like this in many a moon!"

Michael grinned contentedly and ladled another helping onto his plate. "We eat like this all the time, gentlemen."

"I only have one question for you, Michael."

"What's that, Sam?"

"How do you stay so skinny?"

"Just took after my pa, I guess."

"Well, you men, can go sit by the fireplace and talk. The girls need to wash the dishes and clean the kitchen, and I need to take care of Abby. Pa, I will bring her in for you and John to see before I put her to bed."

When she came back, she noticed that Sam was asleep in the rocking chair. John and Michael were talking quietly. She whispered, "All the excitement must have tired him out."

Sam stirred and opened his eyes. "Just restin' my eyes. Let me see my new granddaughter. I won't hold her, but I want to get a look at her."

John came over by Sam and touched the baby's downy, dark hair. "She's a pretty little thing. She makes me think of you when you were a baby, Milly."

"Do you remember what I looked like, John?"

"Sure, I do. I was four years old when Pa brought you out to meet me and Will. You had the same solemn eyes and the same thick, black hair this little girl has. Remember, Pa, I asked you if I could play with my baby sister?"

"Yes, and I told you to wait until she was bigger."

"That's right. And I remember Will said, 'Why do you want to play with that little baby? She's no fun.'"

"Guess he didn't like me, even then."

John chuckled. "Don't feel bad. He never liked me neither."

Sam took another long draw on his pipe and let it out slowly. "Will is my son, so I will always love him, but I don't care for his wife."

She shook her head. "So, you finally admit it? All I can say is, I am surprised you stayed in the same house with her all those years."

"I spent a lot of time fishin' in the river or huntin' in the woods. If I had to be inside, I mostly stayed in my room and read."

Michael, looking pensive, spoke up. "I guess you didn't have an easy time with my mother either, did you, Amelia?"

"No, I didn't, but we weren't there a really long time, and I have always liked your pa."

"Everybody likes Pa. He's never had an enemy in his life."

Sam nodded in agreement. "Yes, Josh Stone is a good man."

She stifled a yawn. "This little girl needs to get some rest, and so do I. John, I hope you don't mind sleeping with Pa."

"I don't care as long as he can put up with my snorin'."

Sam grinned. "I probably won't hear you over my own buzz saw."

"All right. I better make sure the kids are all in bed. Stay up as long as you want. Goodnight."

"Good night, Milly."

"Sleep good, sis."

THE THREE MEN sat quietly after Amelia left until Michael broke the silence. "Today at the store, I heard somebody talk about not havin' a job to feed his family, so they was havin' a Hoover Hog for supper again. Of course, he was talking about eatin' a rabbit he had shot hisself. Things are pretty bad when people start makin' jokes about the President and the Depression."

Sam lowered his pipe. "The way I see it, this place has always been in a depression of some kind."

"Well, some of the papers tell us that the economy is improvin', and the Great Depression will be endin' soon."

"Maybe it will end in New York or Washington, D.C., but I agree with Pa. Things around here stay about the same. Thousands of our people are pourin' into California, trying to find work to feed their families, but most of them wind up comin' back home in worse shape than when they left."

Michael took some tobacco from a sack, lying on a small table near his big, overstuffed chair, and poured it carefully into his pipe. He offered the sack to John, who waved it away.

After lighting his pipe, he looked up at John. "Then there's men like Arthur O'Dell, who, with his family, bounces back and forth between California and here, makin' money pickin' fruit for the big farms, and comin' home at the end of the season. They stay here until the money is spent. Then they're on the road to California again. I don't want to live that way myself, and that's no way to raise kids, draggin' them around all over California, never givin' them a chance to get an education or make friends. But how about you? Ain't you ever thought of goin' to California?"

"Never saw the need. You just go about a hundred or so miles from here, and you can find a good job and an easier life. That's what I been doin' for the last fifteen years, makin' money in the oil fields of Tulsa and thereabouts, savin' it up, so I could come back here and farm again.

"If you was makin' such good money, why did you come back to this poor place?"

Sam chuckled. "I suspect it's for the same reason that I have stayed here my whole life, ain't it, John?"

Michael stopped smoking his pipe and raised his eyebrows. "Why's that?"

"Because, as poor as it is, it's still home."

"That's right, Pa."

"Well, you fellers, stay up as long as you want, but this old man's gotta get some rest."

"As soon as I finish this pipe, I'll be hittin' the hay myself. Do you all need anything?"

John shook his head. "Nah, we're fine, Michael. Thanks again for your hospitality."

"Don't mention it. You're kin."

John got up early the next morning, dressed, and put his hand on the back door. He turned and saw Amelia, walking into the kitchen.

"Did you even sleep?"

"Of course, I did. Remember I went to bed before you men?"

"Not that much earlier. Don't worry about fixin' me breakfast. I'll just grab some cornbread and a cup of buttermilk, and I'll be on my way."

"It will just take a minute to fix you some ham and eggs. I even have some biscuits left and coffee left over from yesterday morning. I'll warm them up in a jiffy. A hard-working man needs a hearty breakfast."

"All right. You don't have to twist my arm! I will stay a little longer and eat."

She poured a big cup of coffee for John and a smaller one for herself. "I think I'll eat a bite with you so I can enjoy the quiet before the kids get up. Do you really think Pa is going to be all right?"

"I believe he is gettin' older and weaker. Colds hang on more now with him. That's one reason I came home."

"What are the other reasons?"

"I missed home."

"Anything else?"

"Yes, but promise you won't tell?"

She put a hand to her mouth to hide her smile. "Are we ten and six again? All right. I won't tell."

"I want to get married and start a family before I get too old. You know, I will turn forty-three next year."

She looked at John's serious face and laughed. "Oh, is that all? I thought as wrinkled and gray-headed as you are, you must be seventy!"

"So, I'm a Cherokee. I know I don't look old, but my muscles and joints tell me I'm gettin' there."

She swatted his arm. "Well, old man, I think getting married is a wonderful idea. You will have to come to church with us and take a look at the single ladies."

"If anyone will have me."

"Oh, we'll find someone for you. Don't you worry."

When John arrived back at the house that night, he was dirty, hungry, and tired. After he cleaned up, he sat at the supper table and ate.

Sam waited until John was almost finished. "How was the house?"

"There's a lot to be done. It's goin' to take a lot longer than I thought, and I am goin' to have to ask for some help."

Michael put down his fork and spoon. "Sure, John, what do you need? Me and the boys can help."

"So can I."

"Not this time, Pa. I need help in fixin' the roof. If we don't get it fixed soon, the rain will get in and damage the walls and the floor. The other stuff I can do by myself, mostly just nailin' boards and cleanin' the place up. Michael, do you think you, myself, and Clay can fix the roof on Saturday?"

"Don't leave Ross out. He's as nimble as a monkey and can climb like a mountain goat. Yep, if we put our minds to it, the four of us can get it done Saturday. I 've got some old shingles and boards in the barn you are welcome to."

"No, I want to pay you for them."

"Don't worry about it, man! You will be doin' me a favor to haul it off out of my way."

Amelia didn't like being left out. "Well, I can't do much physical labor, but tomorrow I will cook some extra food for you to take for lunch on Saturday. I can fry up a couple of chickens, fix a big bowl of potato salad, and bake some biscuits and pies. I will send Susan and Emily to help with the cleaning."

"That all sounds mighty good, sis. I appreciate all that you and Michael are doin' for me and Pa."

Michael waved his hand. "Think nothin' of it. You're family."

The children were excited when their father told them about their workday on Saturday. "Sounds like a picnic!" Clay rubbed his hands in anticipation.

Ross sneered. "You're just happy that you get a lot to eat. I'll have fun climbin' on Grandpa's roof."

"It will be nice just to go somewhere else for once."

Emily said, "Susan, what do you mean by that? We go to church every Sunday."

"That's not the same. Who knows? We might even go through town."

Ross mimicked Susan's voice. "Who knows? I might even see Tommy *Swimmer!*"

"You little brat! You quit teasin' me!"

"Or what?"

"Or I will give you what for!"

Susan grabbed for Ross, but he danced nimbly out of her reach, just as Amelia entered the room. "Susan, if you do that again, you will stay home Saturday, and Mary will go in your place."

"Yes, Ma."

As soon as their mother left the room, Ross stuck his tongue out at Susan.

She whispered, "You just wait!"

THE SATURDAY WORKDAY was warm and sunny. The children were delighted that Michael stopped by their grandfather's store to borrow Josh's pickup truck. Josh came out and handed them all a lollipop. "Here you go, kids! You deserve these 'cause you're goin' to work hard today."

The children all yelled, "Thanks, Grandpa."

He grinned, squeezed Clay's shoulder, and ruffed Ross's hair.

Susan asked in her sweetest voice, "Pa, can me and Emily ride in the back of the truck?"

"I guess so."

As Susan climbed out of the wagon, she issued an order. "You boys stay in the wagon."

"We'll see. Pa, can me and Clay ride in the truck, too?"

"All right. Just be quick about it."

Ross gave Susan a triumphant look as he climbed into the back of the truck.

John had been listening to the kids' conversation. He assumed his saddest expression. "Don't nobody want to ride with me anymore?"

"I'll ride with you, Uncle John. You would think they ain't never seen a truck before."

"Tell you what, Clay. Since you stuck with me, I'll let you handle the horses."

"Thanks, Uncle John. I would take a horse over a truck any day."

"We think alike, my boy."

AMELIA MET THE work party at the door that night. "My, what a scruffy-looking lot!" She frowned when she saw Ross's bruised face.

Before her mother could ask, Emily offered an explanation. "Ross fell and landed face down on a rock."

"Oh, really? Is that what happened, Ross?"

Ross hesitated, looked at Susan's grim face, and said, "Yeah."

"Well, everyone wash up, and come back to the supper table. That is, if you're hungry. You might still be full from all the lunch I sent."

John grinned at Clay. "Oh, I think we can eat, can't we, Clay?"

"Yes, sir!"

Even though she was usually exhausted, Amelia was happier when Sam and John were at her house. It took her by surprise that, on a day when she was feeling content, she lost all control. On that terrible day, her anger was directed at Clay, as usual. One warm spring Saturday evening, Mary, Emily, and Susan were taking their weekly bath in the large tin stock tank, which served as the family bathtub. Even though the tub, for convenience sake, was located outside, Michael had erected a large, encircling wooden screen to give family members a measure of privacy. The girls were splashing and playing happily when suddenly little Mary let out a squeal. "Ma, Clay's looking at us!"

Her sisters tried to shush her, but it was too late. Amelia came out and caught a glimpse of Clay's back as he tried to make his getaway. What she didn't see was that Ross had already run away. Slow Clay didn't get away in time.

She screamed, "You, dirty, filthy boy!" She grabbed a broken tree branch and brought it down on Clay's back, shoulders, legs, everywhere, again and again. She didn't hear the girls' pleas for mercy. She didn't hear Clay's shuddering gasps of pain. She didn't see the blood as it poured from the gaping wounds she had inflicted on her son.

And she didn't know when Michael came up behind her and grabbed the stick from her hand. "For God's sake, woman! Do you want to kill the boy? Stop it!"

In a blind rage, Amelia replied, "The dirty boy deserved it! He was lookin' at his sisters' nakedness, like an animal!"

"Nobody deserves what you did to him. He's just a boy, Amelia. All boys try to look at girls sometimes. That's just the way they are. Emily, put some clothes on and help your brother clean himself up."

Amelia would never forget the look of pure hatred that Clay gave her as he limped from the yard. She turned around and saw that Sam and John had accompanied Michael to see what was happening. Her father turned a shocked, pained face toward her for minute and then went back to his room. John got on his horse and left the house.

V

JOHN & SAM

JOHN WASN'T SURE where he was going. He just knew he had to get away from what he had just witnessed at his sister's house. If any man had said, "Your sister is a mad woman," he would have slugged him or at least argued against the statement. But today, Amelia had shown a side of herself he had never seen before, standing there, with her loosened hair streaming over her shoulders, her face flushed, and her eyes black with rage, whipping her own son until the blood ran down his back. If Michael or someone hadn't stopped her, she might have beat the life out of young Clay. The sight disturbed and sickened him, and all he could think of was getting away from his sister and her cruelty. He had no destination in mind, so he gave his horse its head. It wasn't long until he realized he was traveling toward his old house.

Arriving there, he dismounted, patting his steed about the head and shoulders. "Good, Soldier. You knew where to bring me. Let me make you comfortable and give you some supper."

John moved things out of his way as he walked through the house. All he really needed to do was finish up his carpentry projects, clean the place up, and haul off the trash, maybe buy some furniture, like a used bed for his father to sleep on. Another two weeks at the most, and Pa could move back in. He was ready. He could tell that by the disgusted expression Pa had on his face when he saw what Amelia had done. Michael had the same look, disgusted and something else—hatred? Or maybe it was just sadness he felt that his wife, the mother of his children, could be angry enough to beat her own son. John wasn't sure exactly what Michael's expression meant, but he knew it didn't bode well for his sister or her marriage.

BACK AT THE Stone house, Sam's manner toward Amelia had undergone a great change. He remained courteous and appreciative, but the warm feeling of comradery was gone. The children were still his chief delight, especially little Zachary and Mary, with whom he played hide and seek endlessly. He just never had much to say to Amelia anymore.

He seemed to go out of his way to be kind to Clay, inviting the boy to go on long walks with him around the property. He was also teaching the older children Cherokee. Ross, who didn't like school, had always had a talent for mimicry and picked up the language in record time, which delighted Sam.

In eleven days, Sam left to live with John, amidst tears from little Zack and repeated hugs from Mary. She pleaded with him. "Please don't go, Grandpa. If you go, we won't have nobody to play with."

He drew her close for a big hug. "I will come see you most every Sunday, and you can get your pa to bring you over anytime."

Amelia's heart sank when he left her out. "Now, Pa, are you sure that you want to move now? We could still have some cool nights, and that old house is very drafty. You finally got rid of your cough, and I would hate to see you get it back."

"Milly, you and your family have been real good to me, but I don't want to overstay my welcome. No, it's time for me to join John. I may be old, but I can still help him around the house and with his garden and stock. Tell the older kids goodbye for me. I will be here after church Sunday for dinner, if that's all right."

"I will be expecting you. Take care of yourself."

ON THE WAY home, Sam and John talked. "Thanks for takin' me home with you. I needed to get out of there before I told Amelia what I thought of her."

"I know, Pa. Do you think Clay will be all right?"

Sam sighed. "I think so. He's stayin' away from his mother, but he won't ever forgive her for what she done to him. And maybe Michael won't, either."

"I know. That's what I'm afraid of."

The next day was Saturday, and John and Sam were sitting on the front porch, finishing their coffee, when they heard a wagon approaching. Sam shielded his eyes against the morning sun. "Can you tell who it is?"

"Looks like Michael. He's by himself."

Michael brought the buggy to a halt and walked up to the porch. "John, I was wonderin' if you'd like to go to Sallisaw with me today."

"I might. What's your business?"

"There's a man named Cain Bighorse who has a horse I want to look at. I need you to go with me."

"I don't mind goin', but why do you need me?"

"Cain is a full-blood and only speaks Cherokee. He won't even deal with anybody who can't understand him."

"All right. Let me take care of some things first, and I'll go with you."

Sam spoke up. "Guess I ain't too old to milk and feed a few cows and chickens. Go on. If you wait too long, Cain might sell that horse to somebody else."

"Thanks, Pa. All right, Mike. Guess I'm ready to go."

MICHAEL KEPT UP a running discourse on the sights they encountered. He stopped and pointed. "Somebody told me over that way is the remains of Sequoyah's old cabin and salt works. Amelia's been after me to take her and the kids there to look around, but I ain't got around to it yet."

John looked in the direction Michael pointed. "They would probably enjoy that. Maybe I'll take Pa there someday. I think he would like it."

When they got to Wild Horse Mountain, Michael said, "Ever been here before?"

"Nope. Just hope you know where you're goin'."

"I been here a time or two, so I think we're all right."

The stories about Cain Bighorse were true. He folded his huge arms and grunted when Michael said, "Heard you had a horse for sale."

When John repeated the question in Cherokee, he started talking. Yes, he had three horses for sale, a mare, a filly, and a gelding. Which one were they wanting to buy?

After a brief consultation with Michael, John said, "The gelding. Can we see him?"

Michael ran his hands over the horse's body and opened his mouth to examine the teeth. "Looks strong and sound. Ask him if he can run."

When John asked, Cain laughed, waved his hands, and made whooshing sounds. "Said he could run like the wind."

Michael chuckled. "I kinda figured that's what he said. How much?"

After going back and forth, Cain and Michael decided on a price and shook hands. Michael counted out the money, and Cain handed the horse's reins to him.

Michael spoke softly to the horse, put a saddle on him, and was soon comfortably seated. "John, you can follow us over to the Sallisaw Inn. I'll buy your dinner, and we can talk."

WHEN THEY GOT to the inn, Michael said, "The food here is good, and they give you plenty."

"That's what I like to hear. It's been a long time since breakfast. How do you like your new horse?"

"He's a dandy. Can't wait to get him someplace where I can see how fast he really is. All right. Let's eat."

They had arrived late in the afternoon, so the place wasn't crowded. "Sit down right here, John. They'll be somebody to wait on us pretty soon."

The heavily made-up woman threw her hands up when she saw Michael. "Mikey, is that you? It's been so long since I seen your pretty face that I thought you forgot all about me!"

"Jewel, how could I ever forget about you? Come here and meet my friend, John."

"Why, hello, John! You're a handsome one. You want me to find a pretty lady to keep you company?"

John tried to keep a poker face. "No, that's all right, ma'am. I just want to eat a good meal and get on my way.'

"Suit yourself." Jewel turned her full attention to Michael. "Now, tell me what you've been up to and why I haven't seen you in almost two years."

John listened to the painted woman prattle on and on. He was glad when his big steak arrived, and he had something to do besides listen to her talk. Why had Michael brought him here? Having finished eating several minutes before Michael and his lady friend, he pushed away his empty plate and stood up. "I need some air."

Michael stood up and turned to Jewel. "Go ahead and finish eatin', honey. I'll be back in a few minutes." He followed John outside.

ONCE OUTSIDE, JOHN turned his fury on Michael. "What are you doin' with that woman, Mike? Did you forget you're married?"

Michael sighed. "No, I can't ever forget that, John, but sometimes I would like to. You seen how your sister acted, and that wasn't the first time. It's hard livin' with someone who gets crazy mad all at once or sulls up and won't talk for weeks on end. Most the time she acts like she can barely stand me touchin' her. You ain't never been married, so you don't know how it is."

"I don't know, but I do know what you're doin' ain't right."

"No, it ain't right, and I try not to do it, but sometimes, I just got to go somewhere where a woman is glad to see me and wants me to touch her."

John sneered. "Glad to see your money, you mean."

"Maybe so, but tonight for a little while I can laugh and forget about Amelia and her madness. I'll be home in the mornin'. I would appreciate it if you just take the horses back to my house and tell the boys to take care of them. You can ride one of the old nags home. We can pick her up next time we come over."

"What should I tell Amelia?"

"If she asks, tell her I stayed over at the Bighorse place, because Cain asked me to stay, and I didn't want to insult him."

"All right, but I hate lyin' to my sister."

"It's better than hurtin' her with the truth."

JOHN PURPOSELY TOOK the long way home so everyone would be in bed at Amelia's house. He took care of the horses himself and stowed the buggy in the barn.

The next morning, he made his excuses to his father. "Pa, I don't feel so good. Probably somethin' I ate at Sallisaw yesterday. You can get yourself to church, can't you?"

"Why sure."

He was glad that Amelia never asked him why Michael spent the night at Sallisaw.

In the months ahead, John and Sam continued to develop and improve their property. More Saturdays than not, John would drive his buggy over and say, "Sis, I hate to ask you again, but could I borrow Clay and Ross to help around my place?"

Most of the time she agreed unless Michael had his own plans that included the boys. She frowned a little when they seemed so eager to go, especially Clay.

ONE SUNDAY, JOHN didn't sit with them in their family pew. He moved to the back of the church to sit by a young widow, Sally Christie. Ross scowled and complained. "Why is Uncle John sittin' by her?"

Susan, who was involved in her own first romance, defended John's actions. "Hush, Ross. Uncle John can sit wherever he wants to."

After church John stopped Amelia and her family as they started to leave the church, "Amelia, I know this is short notice, but could I bring Sally to Sunday dinner today at your place?"

Amelia smiled broadly at John and Sally. "Of course. Sally, you are welcome to come with John. We look forward to getting to know you better."

"Thanks, Missus Stone. I am sorry I didn't cook anything to bring."

"Don't worry yourself about that. We always have more than enough. Pa, why don't you ride with us in the truck and let John bring Sally in the buggy?"

"Sure. Sorry to scoot you out of the front, Susie."

"That's all right, Grandpa. I don't mind."

Bold Ross spoke up, "No, she likes it better because Tommy Swimmer can see her better in the back."

Amelia scolded him. "Ross, don't get something started again. Pa, I have a feeling you will get a new daughter-in-law very soon."

"That'll be all right, but I may be spendin' more time at your place."

Little Mary, bouncing on her grandpa's knee, yelled, "Whee!"

AMELIA'S SPIRITS ROSE as she saw her father's coldness

toward her dissipate more and more as the months went by. She made a promise to Michael and herself to never lose control again. Clay remained distant and cool to her but warm and friendly toward everyone else in the family.

Busy days flew by until it was time for Susan's graduation from Jubilee High School. Amelia had made her a new floral cotton dress for the occasion. After Susan put it on, and Emily helped her braid her long sandy hair into a neat bun, she took a long look at her eldest child. "Oh, my!"

"What is it, Ma?"

"You look just like your Aunt Susan! And you look so grown-up!"

"That's good, isn't it?"

"It's good that you look like Susan, but it's not good you are almost grown."

Amelia took a handkerchief from her apron pocket and wiped her eyes.

Susan stared closely at her mother. "Ma, are you cryin'?"

"Just a little."

"Can I ask you something?"

"What's that?"

"Can I work at Grandpa Josh's store?"

"Maybe you can do that part-time this summer, but you will start college at Tahlequah in the fall."

"What if I don't want to go to college?"

"Of course, you will go to college, but we will talk more about it later. Now, girls, help me get the little ones ready."

MICHAEL SQUEEZED AMELIA'S hand when Susan walked across the stage and received her diploma. "She looks just like my sister, Susan."

"I know."

Sam nodded his head. "And all the young men are lookin' at her."

"I know, Pa."

"Then you know you won't get to keep her much longer."

The next month was John and Sally's wedding. While everyone was congratulating the bride and groom, Sam told them, "I packed my suitcase, and I'm goin' to stay with Milly for a while."

Sally protested. "You don't have to do that!"

"Yes, I do. It will give you some time to get used to bein' husband and wife."

John, looking handsome and young in his new suit, smiled and stared at his beautiful young bride, dressed in the blue silk dress that was his wedding gift to her. "That's not a bad idea, Pa. Thanks."

SAM'S SHORT VISIT turned into an extended stay over the next few months. Then it was fall again, and one Saturday he took Mary and Zack out in the woods to gather colorful leaves. Mary ran ahead with a basket, picking up pretty leaves. "Hey, little *jis-tu,* don't get too far ahead of us."

"I'm not a rabbit, Grandpa."

"What are you then?"

"I'm a girl."

"A baby girl?"

"No, a big girl!

Little Zack yelled, "Me, too! I big, too!" as he struggled to get away from Sam's firm grip.

"No, you don't, Zack, you need to stay with me. Mary, come back!"

But Mary was gone.

"Come on, Zack. We gotta look for Mary. She can't have gone far."

Sam stepped out of the woods into a meadow. Across the meadow, the land dropped into a ravine through which ran a small creek. He picked up Zack and hurried to the ravine. "Mary, you better not be in that creek!"

But she was.

HE SAW HER below, splashing and struggling to stay afloat. Sam dropped a surprised Zack at the top of the ravine. "You stay here!"

Sam scrambled down the ravine to where Mary was. "Mary, kick your legs and move your arms. I'm comin'."

He threw himself into the cold water and swam to where she was. It had been raining a lot, so the water was over his head. He grabbed Mary by her long brown hair and pulled her through the water.

When they emerged from the water, they were both shivering uncontrollably. Sam hugged the child. "Don't you ever do that again!"

AS THEY TRUDGED home, Sam took big breaths and tried to calm his racing heart.

Amelia was looking out the window when she saw them coming. Seeing their wet, cold state, she brought out warm blankets and wrapped them up. "Pa, go into your room and get you some dry clothes on! Mary and Zack, come with me!"

Mary trembled and cried out, "Don't whup me, Ma!"

"Silly girl! No one's getting punished. We'll talk more about it later. Let's find you some dry clothes."

When Zack heard Mary cry, he started wailing, too. "Hush, the both of you. Now quit crying. You're all right."

Mary recovered nicely, but Sam's cough returned and hung on for a week. He could barely walk across a room without getting winded. He said, "I just took a dunk in cold water, and the cold settled in my lungs," to explain his weakened condition. After much protesting, Amelia persuaded him to allow Michael to take him to Tahlequah to see the doctor.

HE BROUGHT HER father home that afternoon before the kids were home from school. Amelia could tell by their faces the news wasn't good.

"What did Doctor Jamison say?"

"He said I likely had a heart attack, but I will be all right."

"Tell her all of it, Sam."

Sam sighed. "He said that I am goin' to have to spend a lot of time in bed, restin'."

"Well, that's what you will do then."

Amelia and her father got closer in the following months. He told her family stories and stories about his life and answered all her questions. Once she asked him, "If you admired Redbird Smith so much, why didn't you become a Nighthawk or a Keetoowah?"

"Two reasons. First, my ma and pa were set on me getting an allotment. Pa would say, 'What fool turns down free land?'"

He paused and looked off into space for some time.

"And two?"

"I met Mary Elk."

"What did Ma have to do with it? Best I remember, Ma was pretty and very quiet."

"Well, she was always pretty, but she wasn't always quiet. She was the prettiest girl at church, and all the young men wanted to court her, kinda like Susan."

"What was her family like?"

"Oh, they was good people, but there was a lot of clan family members, livin' together, and not much money to go around. To top it off, they were Nighthawks, and her father and brother wouldn't hear of doin' anything that might make their lives easier. Somehow, Mary managed to look like a princess anyway, but she didn't like bein' poor. I think that's one reason she let me court her. My family was fairly prosperous. We had a large farm and could afford farm hands to help work it. We didn't have a lot of cash money, but there was always plenty to eat and a good place to live. It wasn't too long after I met her that Pa told me, 'If you let that one go, you'll live to regret it!'"

"What did Grandma Star say?"

"She said, 'Mary is Cherokee, pretty, and smart. She's perfect for you!'"

"And Granny Bluebird?"

"She never met Mary. She died three years before Mary came into my life, but I know she would have approved of her. We only had one problem between us, and that was Redbird Smith and the Nighthawks."

"I take it she didn't like him."

"Oh, she liked him all right, personally, and had me take her to several of his stomp dances near Vian. You know the place. You went with John and me there once."

"Yes, I remember."

"She didn't like his ideas. She said, 'Think of it this way. The whites took our land and homes. Now they feel guilty about it and want to give part of it back, legally. Why shouldn't you take what they owe you?'"

"But you know what? After Will and John was born, she decided she wanted her brother to teach them how to be good clan members and Nighthawks. She wanted Will to stay with him all summer when he was just seven, and I said 'no' to that. It was one of our few disagreements."

Sam suddenly stopped speaking and took a deep breath. He paused for a full minute before resuming. "Anyway, I am glad I married Mary and glad I took the allotment, even though it was after she passed. I got allotments for all you children and for myself. That's almost six hundred and fifty acres, plus nearly four hundred from the old place, over a thousand acres in all."

"Too bad Will has most of it."

"If I had known how things were goin' to turn out, I wouldn't have deeded most my land over to Will. Too late now. Speakin' of doin' things different, while the kids are all gone, do you have time to take me over to John's this afternoon? There's something I need to get there."

"Sure, if you can manage the horses. I will have to hold Zack and Abigail on my lap."

✳

WHEN THEY GOT to the house, an extremely pregnant Sally greeted them. "I'm glad you came. It gets lonesome around here with John workin' in the fields all day. I made some cinnamon rolls and coffee. Do you want some?"

"That would hit the spot, Sally. When's my grandson due?"

"The first of July."

Amelia chuckled. "Well, Pa. Sounds like this grandchild could share your birthday, but how do you know it will be a boy?"

"Just a feelin' I got."

"Well, those feelings can be wrong. Michael was sure Susan was going to be a boy."

Sally smiled and patted her stomach. "It doesn't matter whether the baby is a boy or girl. All that matters is it's healthy."

After they ate, Sam said, "Sally, would you mind watchin' the little ones for a minute? I need to show Milly somethin' in my room."

"Sure."

A few minutes later, she looked around Sam's tidy room. "So, what is it you want to show me?"

Sam opened a dresser drawer and handed her a small, smooth, red stone. "This is yours now."

She ran her fingers over the stone. "It belonged to Granny Bluebird, didn't it?"

"Yes, that stone came from her old home in Georgia, and she kept it with her over the Trail until she brought it here."

"I know the story, but why do you want to give it to me?"

"It's supposed to go to one of the women of the family."

"Then why do you have it?"

"Because Granny Bluebird said I was the one to have it. She said my mother wasn't very interested in the old ways and the old stories, and I was. You are too, aren't you?"

"Yes, and the older I get, the more interested I am."

"That's good. Oh, one more thing before I give it to you. I want to talk to you about something that might make you a little angry. Just hear me out first, all right?"

She took a deep breath. "All right."

"Amelia, you need to make things right with Clay. He's already talkin' about wantin' to quit school and move off somewhere to work."

She took another deep breath in order to calm her nerves. "He can't do that! He's far too young, and we need him home to help with the work."

Sam stared deep into her worried eyes. "I hear you say that you need him, but do you love him?"

"Pa, why do you ask? Why, I would give my life for any of my children! I love them all with all my heart and soul."

"Yet Clay thinks you hate him."

"I don't hate Clay. Maybe I am harder on the older kids because I depend on them so much, and, yes, maybe I have been the hardest on Clay. There are things about him that I don't like, but I haven't even raised my voice to him in almost two years now."

"Just promise me you will talk to him and make things right soon."

"I will."

"You know what your mother used to say when I got angry with you kids?"

"What?"

"You only get to have them for a short time, so don't mistreat them. Someday you will wish that you hadn't."

"She was a wise woman, wasn't she?"

"Yes, and you are gettin' more like her each day. Here, keep this stone in a safe place and pass it down to someone in the family someday. When it's time, you will know who to give it to."

JOHN'S SON, RILEY Samuel, was born three days after Sam's birthday, on July 7. John hired a photographer to take pictures of his family in various settings. He was especially proud of the one of Sam, still standing straight and strong, at seventy, cradling baby Riley in his arms. About a month later he brought his family over to see Amelia and Sam, and to show them the pictures. "Look, Amelia, I had a copy made for you of Pa and Riley."

"Thank you, John. I love it. These pictures are all so good. Where did you find your photographer?"

"It's Tim Polecat. He's set up a shop in Tahlequah on Main Street."

Sam spoke up, "I have an idea. What would you think of me hirin' the same photographer and have him come here for some family reunion pictures?"

"That's a fine idea, as long as Penelope doesn't come."

"Seems like I heard the preacher say we are supposed to forgive those who sin against us, daughter."

She smirked. "Yes, but he doesn't know Penelope."

"Well, it would make your old pa happy if he could see all his children in one place for one day, Milly."

Michael took her hand and squeezed it. "You should do it, Milly,"

She opened her mouth to argue but saw her father's hopeful eyes and relented. "All right, but I'm not inviting her myself."

"We'll take care of that, sis."

On September 26, the house was clean, and many tempting dishes sat on Amelia's table. Penelope and Sally brought several dishes, too. "Boys, go get a table out of the smoke house and set it up beside the kitchen table."

"Yes, boys, listen to your father, and Susan, go out and make sure they clean if off before they bring it in here."

After everyone had stuffed themselves on fried chicken, hot biscuits, and several fresh vegetable dishes, Amelia asked, "Is anybody ready for dessert? I made a big peach cobbler and some fried pies, and Penelope and Sally both brought cakes."

Sam groaned. "Give me a few minutes. It all looks good, but I'm full as a tick."

Clay kept his eyes on the table. "Is it all right if I have some of all four?"

Amelia bit back a rebuke and smiled instead. "Of course, you can, Clay. This is a special day, and we want you to enjoy it."

After the meager leftovers were put away, and the pictures were taken. Amelia looked for a place to sit. There was one empty chair beside Penelope, who called out, "Come over, sit, and rest a minute, Amelia. You look plumb tired out."

She didn't really want to sit by Penelope, but she looked into Penelope's small green eyes, made smaller by the fat rolls that surrounded them, and saw nothing but friendly concern. "All right. It might feel good to sit for a minute."

She didn't talk much, but she found she could half-listen to Penelope's rambling conversation, and Sally attended to her advice on childcare and housekeeping. She experienced a feeling of peace and realized it came from obeying her father when he asked her to bring the family together. The kids were all laughing and playing games together. Will and Penelope only had two at home now, a girl, Barbara, who was near Emily's age of sixteen, and the youngest and only son, Douglas, who had just turned eleven and enjoyed playing horseshoes with his cousins and uncles. Their two older daughters were married, and Rosemary was expecting her first baby. Barbara went off with Susan and Emily to the girls' room, no doubt talking about boys and fashion. Best of all, Sam sat in the middle of all of it, holding Riley, and laughing at Mary, Zack, and Abigail's antics. He looked happy, and that made Amelia happy. Yes, it was a very good day, and they might do it again sometime in the future.

After everyone had gone home, Sam patted Amelia on the shoulder and said, *"Wa-do.* Today was the best gift you could ever give me."

THE NEXT TIME everyone got together was eight months later at Sam Clay's funeral. Tall, strong Clay asked John if he could be a pallbearer at his grandfather's funeral. "I told him he could, sis. It seemed real important to him, and he's as big and strong as most of the other pallbearers, even if they are full-grown men, and he's not quite fifteen."

She agreed, but looking at Clay's stricken pale face, as he walked past her, with his grandfather's casket on his shoulders, she wondered if she had made a mistake. He had loved Sam Clay deeply, and it was taking all he had to keep from breaking down. As he passed, she reached out her hand to touch his shoulder, but he gently brushed her hand away. Less than a minute later, Michael reached out his hand, and Clay briefly grasped it in his own before resuming his sad duty.

She tried hard to be kinder to Clay, but she never asked him to forgive her for her earlier bad treatment of him. She thought it would stir up too many painful memories for both of them. As for Clay, he spoke to his mother only when necessary.

VI
BONITA

WHEN BONITA CRIED, Grandma said, "Hush that bawlin', child. Did you think I was goin' to raise you forever? It's your pa's place to do some of it."

She smiled and patted Bonita's hand. "You can still come and see me. It's not like you was goin' miles away."

Twelve-year-old Bonita McKindle, with her big fawn eyes, shiny chestnut hair, early budding figure, and laughing, easy ways, was popular with both boys and girls at her school. She loved school and her life. Today everything changed. Today her father, Anderson McKindle, drove up to Grandma Della's house and said he was taking Bonita home with him to keep house since she was old enough to be useful now.

Bonita thought Della would protest, but instead she calmly said, "It will be a little while until she can get her things together."

In shocked disbelief, Bonita brushed away her tears and didn't say a word until they reached the dirty shack that was now her home. As soon as she had set her cardboard box, which contained all her belongings, down in the kitchen, she made her escape.

"Gotta go to the outhouse!"

Sitting on a stump outside the outhouse, she cried her heart out for loneliness for her grandma and pity for herself. For the most part, Bonita had been happy with Grandma. Now that she was big enough to primp and keep herself clean and neat, she didn't have to face the teasing at school anymore or the sympathetic looks older girls once gave her. She recalled their hurtful words. "That little Bonita would be so pretty if someone would just clean her up."

From that day on, Bonita kept herself neat and tidy, even if it meant sponging off in cold well water with a bar of Ivory soap every morning before she went to school. She brushed the rats' nests out of her thick hair before she went to bed at night and again in the morning. She scrubbed her few garments again and again on the scrub board until they were completely clean. Grandma could never see well enough to get all the spots out. She begged Grandma to buy her a toothbrush at the Stones' store until Della finally gave in. But first she was required to listen to Grandma's arguments against the purchase. It is a foolish waste of good money. Bonita acts like her father's side of the family, prone to giving herself airs. She listened respectfully and thanked Grandma profusely when she handed her the toothbrush. Bonita faithfully brushed her teeth morning and night with Della's bitter-tasting baking soda.

The simple things she had taken for granted like baking soda, a scrub board, and even a bar of Ivory soap were likely missing from her father's house. Now she would never feel comfortable or clean again.

When she got back to the house, father and son were listening to the radio, one of their few luxuries. As soon as Bonita sat down to join them, her father said, "Girl, you better git started on them dishes."

Making as much noise as possible, Bonita went through the few pots stored in the cabinets until she found a big one for boiling water. She also located a bar of lye soap. Next she went to the well in the backyard, filled up the pot, and set the water to boil on the wood stove while she scrutinized the pile of egg-encrusted plates, dirty cups, and an assortment of equally filthy pots, pans, and eating utensils. While the water heated up, she surveyed the rest of the cabinets. She found a little flour, full of bugs, and clumpy baking powder, salt, and soda. An old can of rancid grease sat on the dirty wood stove. There was nothing fit to cook with.

She almost missed a pretty blue and white sugar bowl, far back in the top cabinet. She wasn't tall enough to reach it, but she resolved to find a chair and see what was in it later. She walked over the few feet that separated the bare front room from the tiny kitchen to where Sid sat on the worn sofa, smoking Pall Malls.

"How long's it been since you done the dishes?"

Sid chortled and winked. "We been savin' 'em for you, sis!"

"Thanks a lot."

Anderson threw a half-smoked cigarette to the floor and stomped it out. "Now don't you be gettin' smart, gal. I'm givin' you a place to stay, and you gotta earn your board and keep."

"What about Sid?"

"Sid needn't be bothered with women's work. You just get busy and wash up them dishes and cook us somethin' to eat."

Bonita slammed down yet another slimy pot into the metal tub of hot water and soap. She had been washing dirty dishes for an hour, and she kept finding more and more of the disgusting things. Some neglected pots had mold growing inside them. She put these aside to be thrown away later when no one was watching. Maybe she should just run away back to Grandma's house. But Grandma hadn't objected when Pa came to take Bonita away. Maybe Grandma didn't love her either. She sure never said she did. Something must be wrong with a girl that nobody loved. Pa ignored Bonita until he wanted her to keep house for him. Even now, he barely looked at her. Sure, he was sad because Ma was dead, but at least he got to love her for almost ten years before she died. Her only daughter knew her for less than a year.

She dunked another grimy skillet in the hot water and thought about what Grandma told her about her parents. She said Pa loved Ma so much that he gave up drinking and spent his government checks on buying some land and paying for a pretty little wooden frame house to be built on it. He even had a white picket fence put all around it, and

Ma made flower beds, which she filled with colorful irises. Of course, now, the house and fence were so broken down and dirty that no one would believe they were once nice. No one would guess there were once flower beds in the yard because weeds had overtaken everything.

Her rail-thin brother, cigarette in hand, came into the kitchen carrying another load of dishes. "Here you go, sis. Found these beside Pa's bed."

"Just what I wanted, more dishes."

Sid's blue eyes sparkled, and he gave her a devilish grin.

"Anything to help." He put the dirty dishes on the table, right on top of a fat cockroach that was crawling across, squashing it flat.

"This place is disgusting!"

"Oh, you'll get used to it. Here, have a cigarette. It might calm your nerves." He pulled a cigarette out of the cellophane package in his shirt pocket and offered it to her.

"No, thanks. Those nasty things make me cough."

"Well, suit yourself. I'm goin' to ride over to the store to get me a soda pop. Then I'll probably go and see some friends of mine. See you at supper time. Sure hope it's worth eatin'."

Bonita watched him throw his lanky form onto the shiny red bicycle that was lying on the front porch and peddle quickly away.

"Why, no, I don't want a soda pop or a new bicycle to ride around." She laughed at her own joke, as she threw another slimy plate into the soapy water.

If only her mother were alive, things would have been different. Grandma had told her lots of stories about Ma. Her mother came to Granny's house one time, after she had been married for almost five years, and she was crying because she couldn't get pregnant.

Grandma said, "I told her it might be for the best since she was a frail little thing. 'Course she wouldn't listen to me and went to an Indian midwife with a reputation for helpin' women get in the family way. It must have worked because she delivered Sid about a year later. Ella almost died that time, and the doctor said she mustn't have another baby, but two years later, she had you."

Bonita still remembered the dark, sad feeling which flooded her young heart. In a small quiet voice, she asked, "Did I kill my mother?"

Grandma's dark brown eyes grew sad, and her mouth trembled a little. Bonita sobbed and attempted to climb into Grandma's lap for comfort, but her undemonstrative grandma said, 'Nita, you're smotherin' me again. Sit here beside me and let me tell you somethin'."

She took Bonita's hand and looked deep into her eyes. "Listen to me now. No, you didn't kill your mother. It was Anderson. He was told your ma shouldn't have no more babies, but he only thought of hisself and pawed at her until she got pregnant again."

She was younger then and accepted whatever Grandma said as the gospel truth. Now she wasn't so sure. She paused in her dish washing. No, she wasn't responsible for her mother's death, but Pa blamed her for it. That's why he couldn't stand looking at her. How was she going to bear living with someone who hated her?

She took the pan of dirty water out to the backyard to throw out. Walking over to the well to draw some more water to do the rest of the dirty dishes, suddenly she stopped. What was the big hurry? Her brother was gone to the store, and her pa was snoring away the afternoon. Yes, she could take a little time to think about her problems.

Should she hate Pa for hating her? Grandma certainly hated him. Bonita discovered that when she first heard the story of how she came to live with Grandma. "Here comes Anderson the mornin' after your sweet mama died. He had you in one arm and was holdin' a bag of bottles and diapers with the other hand. Both of you kids was squallin', Sid, because he missed his ma, and you, because you was hungry and wet."

"All he could say to me was, 'Her name is Bonita. That's what Ella wanted.'

"Before I could say a word, he picked Sid up and was out the door. I got you a clean diaper out of the bag and changed you. But you didn't hush your cryin' until I got some milk into your little belly. I was lucky I had just milked the cow and had milk to warm and put in your bottle."

Bonita remembered feeling sad and angry, but she didn't let on. Instead she asked, "Why did she give me a funny name?"

"I sure don't know where Ella come up with such an outlandish name for a child! When I asked Anderson about it later, he told me Ella read it in a book, and it was Spanish for beautiful. That girl! She was always one for readin'. I don't know what she seen in that Anderson. He can barely write his own name, and Ella taught him that. Your ma was a quiet, smart lady, much too good for Anderson McKindle, but she wouldn't hear me when I tried to tell her. She let his good looks and her soft heart for his affliction blind her good sense.

"But then I'm one to talk. I let your grandpa talk me into leavin' our good farm in Cane Hill and movin' over here, just because he thought we could do better here since we would have more land to farm for less money. How was we to know he would have a stroke in three years' time and not be able to farm anymore? Guess I was just lucky to get anything a'tall out of sellin' almost all the land with the bad times comin' on. I learned the hard way to think things through before formin' a judgment about important matters."

Bonita drew the cold water out of the deep well. She took a big, satisfying drink from the bucket. At least there was a well here, and she didn't have to fetch water from the spring like she did at Grandma's house. She wouldn't have to walk so far to go to the store or school either. Maybe it wasn't all bad. She had to do like Grandma said and use good judgment. Her father ran a monthly bill at the Stones' store. Since there was nothing decent to cook for supper, she would buy what she needed and charge it. Pa wouldn't know until the first of the month when he got his new check and went to pay his bill.

Before she went to the store, she must see what was in the sugar bowl while her pa and Sid couldn't catch her looking. She remembered Grandma kept money in two places. She had a man's leather billfold she carried with her when she went to town. This is where she kept the money she used for their living expenses like groceries and feed for their cow and chickens. At night, Grandma slept with the billfold under her pillow. She also had some hidden money she kept in a cracked, white sugar bowl in a top cabinet. This was where Grandma kept her savings, and where she put most of the money that Anderson gave her every month for keeping Bonita. She had watched her grandma get into the bowl whenever Bonita needed a coat, a pair of shoes, or some other necessity. Maybe Pa used his pretty sugar bowl for a bank, too.

She brought one of the sturdy cane bottom chairs over to the cabinet and stood on it. Reaching above her head, she grasped the heavy bowl and carefully brought it down. After she carried it over to the kitchen table, she took off the lid and counted nearly thirty dollars in mostly change and ones. She took five one-dollar bills and five dollars in change. Since Pa was drunk so much, he probably didn't remember exactly how much he had. He could afford to give her some money, and he owed it to her, anyway, to make up for what he spent on Sid. She put the money in her purse and started the mile walk to the Stones' store.

BONITA STOPPED OUTSIDE the store, checking for signs of Sid or his bicycle. She spotted Ross Stone, the best-looking boy in school, playing kick the can with some boys in front of the store. She smoothed her wild hair down with her hand and gave her face a quick spit bath, wishing she had taken time to brush her hair and at least take a sponge bath. She gave him a quick wave and heard him say, "Go on without me, fellas."

One boy yelled, "Ross has to go talk to his girlfriend!"

Another one started singing, "Ross and Bonita sittin' in a tree ..."

He ignored their taunts and walked to where she was standing. "Hello, Bonita. You just missed Sid. He said you started livin' at his house."

"I am for now."

"Well, that's good. I probably will get to see you more since I'm at my grandpa's store every Saturday."

"I guess so."

"Say, would you like a soda pop? Grandpa lets me have an extra one now and then."

She smiled her prettiest smile. "Sure. Thanks, Ross."

Ross smiled back and opened the door for her.

Ross's grandpa looked up from his ledger when he heard the door open. "Well, good afternoon, Miss Bonita! How are you doin' today?"

She smiled again, showing her dimples. "Why, I'm doin' fine, Mr. Stone, and how are you?"

"Fair to middlin'. Is there anything I can help you with?"

"Oh, I'm fixin' to pick up some groceries for my pa in just a few minutes, but Ross and me are goin' to have soda pops first. Is that all right with you?"

"Why, sure! Ross can treat a pretty girl when he wants to. Ross always gets a lemon pop with peanuts. Is that what you want, too?"

"Yes, please."

He opened the big, refrigerated soda case and handed Ross two ice-cold glass bottles, along with a metal beer can opener. "Just help yourselves to the nuts when you're ready for them. You'll probably want to drink them pops down a bit before you'll have enough room to add them."

"Thanks, Grandpa."

"That's quite all right."

Bonita sipped her soda and talked to Ross while Josh went about his business. Once she saw Ross' older brother, Clay, looking at her, but when she caught his eye and smiled at him, he turned red and looked away. Josh's cranky old wife, Martha, frowned at her and Ross, but they ignored her. After she finished her drink and peanuts, she said, "Thanks for the treat. It was so sweet of you! I gotta get the groceries and get back home."

"You're welcome. Say, do you need some help carryin' your groceries to your house?"

"Well, maybe."

Martha made a show of picking up their pop bottles. "Ross, you need to carry those feed sacks out to Mr. Eagle's wagon."

"All right, Grandma. Bonita, let me know when you're ready to go, and I will carry your groceries."

"All right."

She chose a bag of potatoes, a tub of lard, some flour, corn meal, sugar, dried pinto beans, baking powder, soda, salt, pepper, coffee, and a bar of Ivory soap. She had to find the cow when she got home so she would have milk for potato soup. She had the proper ingredients now to help her make good biscuits. When she had finished her shopping, she asked Josh, "Can I borrow one of your bushel baskets to carry my groceries in?"

"Sure. Go right ahead. It might be a mite heavy for a little gal like you. Ross can help you carry your groceries home."

Martha scowled, and her mouth twisted. "See that you bring it back on Monday."

Bonita knew her smile wouldn't affect Martha, but she smiled anyway. "Thanks, Mrs. Stone, and I will bring it back Monday. Please put this on my father's bill."

Martha silently totaled up the bill and gave her a receipt. Josh frowned at Martha and said, "Thanks for your business, Miss Bonita. Come again."

She filled the basket up with the smaller items, and Ross grabbed the heavy potatoes and flour sack for her. He threw the flour sack over his back and held the potatoes with his right arm.

Clay stopped stocking shelves when he saw his brother struggle. "Here, let me carry one of them."

"I don't remember askin' for your help."

"Well, you're about to drop them taters. Hand them over before you do."

"All right, but I could have managed on my own."

Ross and Bonita walked ahead while Clay followed behind them. They chatted about school, and Ross demonstrated all the bird calls he knew. Clay didn't say anything. When they got to the front door, Ross leaned over and whispered in her ear. "Next time it will just be the two of us."

BONITA REALIZED SHE didn't want the boys to see the inside of her father's dirty house, so she stopped them on the front porch. "Thanks ever so much, Ross and Clay! Just put the groceries right here, and Pa will help me carry them inside."

Clay shrugged his shoulders and walked away.

Ross lingered behind and blew her a kiss. "All right. See you soon, Bonita!"

She waved at Ross as he sauntered away. He waved until he was out of sight. She smiled and hugged herself. Here was another reason this place was better than Grandma's, a chance to have a real boyfriend who would get her soda pop.

It took her three trips to get the groceries into the kitchen. She finished washing the dishes, wiped down the table and cabinets, and fed the chickens. She looked for eggs but only found two good eggs and a lot of rotten ones. No one had gathered the eggs in some time. She found the cow who was bawling to be milked. After milking the cow, she drew some more water out of the well, peeled potatoes, and put a pot of potato soup on to cook. She was sweeping the kitchen when she heard her father go out the backdoor to the outhouse.

When next she saw him, he was watching her make the biscuit dough. "So, when do we eat?"

"Probably another hour."

"A man could starve to death, waitin' on you to cook somethin' to eat."

Her rosy cheeks turned bright red. "I had to clean this filthy kitchen before I could cook anything."

He snorted. "Cleanin' ain't nearly as important as cookin'. You're goin' to have to do a whole lot better, gal, if you're going to sleep under my roof. Now, hush your sassy mouth and get some food on the table, pronto!"

She scowled, but just when she started to spout off, she remembered her resolution to use good judgment. She turned around and doubled her efforts to get supper ready.

Sid came in a few minutes later. "Somethin' sure smells good. Is them biscuits I smell cookin'?"

"Uh-huh. I almost got supper ready."

"We never have biscuits to eat. Sure hope they taste as good as they smell."

Sid and Anderson gobbled down almost the whole pot of soup and the pan of biscuits. They left her one bowl of soup and two fluffy biscuits. After he was finished, Sid grinned and said, "Not bad, sis."

Anderson belched. "Them biscuits would have been better with butter. You should've milked the cow earlier so you could have made some butter to go with them."

She bit her tongue to keep back an angry reply. Instead she washed the dishes again, cleaned the kitchen, and watched Pa get a jug of moonshine off the bottom cabinet shelf and leave by the front door. It would soon be dark, and she was tired. She turned to Sid for help. "Do you know where I am supposed to sleep?"

"There's some extra blankets and pillows somewheres around here. Guess you can find them and make you a pallet on the floor somewhere."

Bonita searched and finally found some blankets and pillows clean enough to sleep on. Since she didn't have privacy, she kept her clothes on except for her shoes, and made herself a kind of nest in the far corner of the kitchen. It was almost dark so she didn't use the new soap and soda to clean-up, and she still couldn't find her brush. It would have to wait until morning. Sid was soon snoring in the room he shared with Anderson. Of course, Sid had his own bed. Not her, though, she had to sleep on the floor like a dog! With Grandma, at least she could sleep in a bed, even if they had to share it.

After crying for a few minutes, she dried and closed her eyes. She knew of a place in town where a cheap used bed could be bought. She would use the money from the sugar bowl to buy one. With any luck, her father would be out drinking or passed out in his bed for some time. When he got around to asking where the bed came from, she would say Grandma gave her some spending money she had used to buy it. Now that she had a plan, she could go to sleep.

THE NEXT DAY was Sunday, and Anderson still hadn't come home. She got up early, fed and milked the cow, fed the chickens, and gathered the eggs. After locating a glass jar with a tight lid, she washed it out, poured in some fresh milk, and shook the jar until a soft butter formed. Now she and Sid would have butter with their warm biscuits. She found some sorghum, which she had overlooked, so they could also have sorghum with their fried eggs, gravy, and biscuits. Since breakfast was big and late, she could get by with cooking a late afternoon meal that would be sufficient for dinner and supper. She finished up by soaking some of the pinto beans she had bought the day before. Beans and cornbread would be fine for supper.

As soon as he finished breakfast, Sid left on his bike again, and Bonita prepared for a bath. She boiled several pots of hot water on the stove, pouring each one into a large tin tub. She wrapped her bar of Ivory into a clean washcloth and lowered herself into the tub for a long, hot, cleansing bath. Getting out, she dried off with the one clean bath towel she had found in the house. She wrapped her naked body in a blanket and brushed out her unruly mane. Being clean always made her feel better.

She found some wash tubs, which she filled with hot water, and washed the blankets she was using as bedding and some dirty towels and sheets. The rest of the afternoon was spent in hanging the laundry on the clothesline, mopping the filthy floors, and cooking pinto beans.

When Sid came back home, she made some skillet cornbread, and they ate together. Since Anderson wasn't home, she felt free to question Sid about their lifestyle.

"When do you think Pa will be back, Sid?"

"No way of tellin'. He could come back tonight, or he might be gone all week. It mostly depends on how drunk he gets and how much money he took with him to spend on more liquor."

"Do you ever go drinkin' with him?"

"When I feel like it, but right now I'd rather stay home and eat."

"Are you goin' to school tomorrow?"

"That depends on how I feel when I get up in the mornin'." He frowned at her. "Why are you askin' so many questions?"

"Just makin' conversation."

"Well, me and Pa don't do a lot of talkin' so that's what I'm used to. Anyway, there's still some daylight left, so I'm goin' to ride over to the creek and take a swim."

"All right. Maybe I will see you around bedtime."

"Maybe or maybe not."

She was tempted that night to sleep in one of the two empty beds that were available. But she settled for sleeping in her nest for one more night. She would buy a bed the next day.

SINCE SHE WAS still by herself, Bonita didn't cook the next morning. She ate a biscuit and a piece of cornbread with sorghum for breakfast and drank some of the milk from the day before. The cow greeted her with a friendly moo, and the chickens came running when they saw her walk their way. After feeding and watering the cow and chickens, she milked the cow and looked for eggs. This time she found six.

Returning to the house, she poured some of the milk into a jar and shook it until it formed a soft butter. Remembering Grandma's admonition to not waste anything, she poured the rest of the milk into a large clean jar. She took both jars to the spring house, which was located a few yards from the house. They would keep cool there. She left the beans and cornbread on the stove in case Anderson or Sid came home hungry.

Bonita stopped by the Stones' store on the way to school and dropped off the basket. From there she walked another mile before arriving at the one-room school she had attended since she was six. She saw Clay tying up his horse to the school hitching post.

"Hello, Clay. Where's Ross?"

"Hello, yourself. Last I seen him, he was over there somewhere." He waved his arm in the direction of the woods.

Ross was standing under one of the big oak trees that bordered the school.

"Hey, Bonita. You wanna play hooky and go to the creek with me today?"

"No, I better not. Miss Parsons depends on me to help with the little kids."

"All right then. Maybe another day?"

"We'll see. They're ringin' the bell, so we better go in."

JUBILEE SCHOOL WAS Bonita's favorite place. After flying through her lessons, she helped Miss Parsons by listening to the younger students read. Sometimes she checked their work and tutored them in the areas that were hard for them. Miss Parsons bragged on her whenever she saw Grandma.

Once she said, "I don't know how I could manage without Bonita. She's a big help to me, and I wouldn't be surprised if she didn't become a teacher herself someday."

Such words gave her a warm, happy feeling, and she daydreamed about becoming a teacher exactly like Miss Parsons someday. Grandma seemed almost embarrassed by the complimentary words and just said, "That's good to hear. Thank you."

But when they left the store, Grandma threw ice water on Bonita's warm feelings. "Now, don't get too uppity. None of our folks ever finished high school, much less college for teachin'. The best you can hope for is to find you a good man to support you and the kids you'll have."

She dismissed the negative memory and leaned closer to the bad-smelling girl who was struggling with learning her times tables. After school, she walked over to the used furniture and hardware store.

MR. CRITTENDEN GREETED her at the door. "What can I help you with, young lady?"

"I might be interested in buyin' a small bed and mattress."

"Well, I have a few. Let me show you where they are."

She examined the beds carefully, making sure they were sturdy, with unbroken box springs, and a clean mattress. Pointing out her selection, she asked, "How much?"

"Let's see. You picked out my best set right there. How about... eight dollars?"

"How about five?"

"Make that six, and we have a deal."

"All right, as long as you will deliver it to my house."

"That can be done. Just tell me where you live."

BONITA WAS GLAD she remained by herself. She spent most of the evening setting up her bedroom in the corner of the kitchen where she had been sleeping. She hammered some nails in the wall and hung up some of the clean sheets as a privacy screen. "That's better. Now I will have a comfortable place to sleep."

Early the next morning, Anderson's voice woke her. "What the devil! What have you rigged up, gal?"

Dressed in a long flannel nightgown, Bonita came out from behind the sheets. "I needed my own bed and place, so I fixed it myself."

"Where did you get the money to buy that bed?"

She forced herself to look him right in the eye. "Grandma gave me some spendin' money to spend as I please."

"That sure don't sound like that tight wad, Della O'Dell!"

"Grandma's not so tight with me."

"Maybe not. It's likely my money she feels free to give away. I ate some of those beans and cornbread you had on the stove last night, but me and Sid will be wantin' breakfast before you go off to school."

Feeling generous because he believed her lie, she smiled and said, "Sure, Pa."

Bonita soon accommodated herself to life with her father and brother. She did what she could to make the house clean and comfortable, and she cooked meals whenever someone besides herself was home. She attended school every day and went to the Stones' store for the next three Saturdays where she talked with Ross while they sipped sodas with peanuts. Once they even found a little time to slip off by themselves for a little innocent romance. Ross was the first boy to kiss her, and he told everyone Bonita was his girlfriend. The girls at school said that Ross was "dreamy" with his jet-black hair, dark eyes fringed by long eyelashes, and slim, sinewy physique.

IT WAS CHECK time again. Anderson roared with anger when he went in to buy chewing tobacco and pay his monthly bill. He was handed a big bill by Martha.

"That aggravatin' girl! I never give her permission to charge nothin' to my bill!"

Ross was there when Anderson paid the bill and told Bonita all about it. "After your pa left, Grandma tried to talk Grandpa into not letting you charge anymore, but you know what Grandpa said?"

"What?"

"He said, 'Her pa paid the bill, so why not let the girl charge? Just makes her life and ours a little better.'"

Bonita knew reliability in meeting bills was one of Anderson's few good attributes, and she was keen enough to never mention her purchases. Even though he said she didn't have permission to charge,

Josh Stone would allow it because he knew the bill would always be paid. Life was good for her except for the nights when Anderson staggered in drunk, surrounded by several of his drinking buddies. He turned belligerent and demanding.

"Gal, fix us somethin' to eat. Now. A man could starve to death in this house!"

She hurriedly peeled and fried potatoes and made some skillet cornbread. She usually had a pot of beans already cooked, so all she had to do was heat them up. After a few months of cooking practice, she could cook simple things fast and well. But sometimes, all her cleverness was not enough. Sometimes, Anderson and Sid disappeared on a drunken binge for days at a time, leaving Bonita to fend for herself.

At times like these, she let the cow and chickens out to care for themselves, packed her clothes and her few other possessions into the large cardboard box, which served as a suitcase, and went to stay with one of her aunts. Her mother came from a big family, but most of her siblings had moved away.

BONITA HAD LIVED with her father and brother for two years and had learned how to adjust herself to the circumstances. On this particular day, Bonita came home on a Friday from school, to find the house cold, from the stove being untended, little food in the cupboards, and her father and brother both gone. She carefully considered which aunt to stay with. She would have preferred to stay with Grandma, but she was visiting her sister, who lived in Arkansas. Aunt Dorothy wasn't expected to survive the stroke she had suffered, and Grandma wanted to be with her when she passed.

Aunt Kate was the best-natured, and she never got upset about having an extra mouth to feed. She always welcomed her with a twinkle dancing in her bright blue eyes and hugged her with thin, pale arms. When she was young, Kate had been called "Ella's flunky" because she was so dedicated to caring for her younger sister. This closeness between Kate and Bonita's mother had given Kate a special place in Bonita's heart.

But the last time she had stayed at Kate's house, her husband, Jed, a hulk of a man, slapped Kate. He accused her of "jawin' with the girl" instead of helping him make his batch of moonshine. Bonita hated Jed and hated being the cause of her aunt's pain. Kate just put a cold washcloth to her cheek, tried to smile, and asked her if she could cook supper and mind the young'uns while she helped Jed. Bonita had cooked a meager supper, washed the dishes, and put the three little ones to bed. She left early the next morning, before anyone was up, to avoid any more trouble for her aunt.

ANDERSON HAD THREE sisters—Coweta, Inez, and Lucinda. Coweta and Inez had married young and left when their husbands, who were brothers, took them to Oregon to live. Bonita only knew them through the letters and pictures they sent every Christmas. Aunt Lucinda, who lived at Park Hill, had been a pretty girl, and her relatives said Bonita resembled her when she was young. Lucinda was smart, smart enough to marry an older, prosperous man, Matthew Webb, who owned a large dairy farm. The house he bought her had once belonged to a prosperous family that had lost their fortune in the Civil War. The two-story house was older than most in the area, but well-built with large rooms and elaborate woodwork. Bonita told all her friends, "It looks a lot like what one of those southern plantations probably looked like in the old days."

Matthew doted on his young bride and wouldn't let her soil her hands with helping him with the farm.

Grandma liked to say, "Matt spoiled a rotten girl into an even rottener woman."

Lucinda didn't have much to do with her family. She tolerated Bonita's presence well enough as long as she tended "Little Matt."

Little Matt was the bright star of Lucinda's life, born eight years after his youngest sister was born and ten years after the oldest, also a girl. As the long-awaited boy, he had been so smothered with attention that he was a holy terror. Bonita was one of the few people who could keep him entertained and happy. The food was good and plentiful at Aunt Lucinda's, and she got to sample treats she seldom enjoyed anywhere else like store-bought candy bars, cookies, and ice cream. Her aunt was a good cook, and she enjoyed stuffing herself with crisp, southern fried chicken, thick cream gravy, hot buttered biscuits, homecanned green beans, fluffy mashed potatoes, and fresh peach cobbler, topped with the store-bought ice cream. No wonder everyone in their family was chubby, especially Aunt Lucinda, whose fancy dresses kept getting larger every year.

The only drawback to staying with her Aunt Lucinda was Little Matt could sometimes be a handful. Bonita bore the child's outbursts for a long time but reached her limit when he kicked her because she dared to rest after chasing "Matthew, the Outlaw" for hours. Bonita responded with a firm smack to Matt's bottom, which was met with wailing from Matt and outrage from his protective mother.

That time she was shown the door promptly and told, "Don't come back until you learn to behave!"

Since Bonita hadn't learned, she knew she had better find another place to stay.

THE BEST CHOICE would be Aunt Esther. In some ways, Esther reminded her of Grandma. She was short, red-haired, freckled, a virtual fireball of energy, but she also could turn sour and mean when angered, with a razor-sharp tongue and on rare occasions, a quick slap for discipline. Esther's oldest daughter, Blythe, was a best friend/enemy to Bonita. Blythe was the same age as she but seemed younger, with her slim, boyish figure, and shy manner. She liked Blythe because she could tell her anything, and it would remain a secret forever.

She also resented her because Blythe held nothing back when she was angry. "At least I have a mother, and my Pa's not a drunk! Why don't you just get that old box from under the bed and leave? You don't belong here."

She told herself Blythe did this out of jealousy because Bonita had so many boy and girl friends at school. But when she brought it up, Blythe would emphatically deny it. "Me? Jealous of you? What is there to be jealous of?"

Actually, she was a little jealous of Blythe, not only because she had a stable home life and Bonita didn't, but because she had a father who loved Blythe and her sisters more than anything in the world. Grandma often told the story of how when Blythe was a toddler she cried and begged her father to catch the moon for her.

She always ended the story with, "And that fool, Wade, climbed up on a stump and stood on his tiptoes to show that spoiled child he couldn't reach it!" Afterwards, she always rolled her eyes to show her surprise that any man could be so foolish in dealing with a small child.

Even Anderson seemed to love Blythe. He was always saying, when he saw Bonita, laughing and carrying on with her friends at the store, "Why can't you be quiet like Blythe? She's just like your sweet mother."

Bonita always answered with the same words. "I ain't Blythe, and I'm glad I ain't!"

Still, except for when she got jealous, Blythe was a good friend to her, and she needed another girl to laugh with and share confidences with. Blythe even let her borrow some of her dresses and shoes sometimes. Bonita loved to look in the mirror at herself in a well-filled new dress and saddleoxfords that weren't scuffed and run-over. So, this time she went to Aunt Esther's and stayed nearly two weeks until the girls started arguing. Aunt Esther got sick of their fussing, slapped both girls, and sent Bonita home.

WHEN SHE OPENED the front door, she gagged. The smell of vomit, excrement, and dirty dishes, left to set for days, permeated the air. She stood with the door in her hand, thinking about walking back out. As she did sometimes when she was alone, she spoke her thoughts aloud. "There's no place for me to go, so I might as well get on with it."

It took her all day, but she went to bed in a clean house. She had eaten the last eggs for supper. Tomorrow after school she would buy some groceries at the Stones' store. Maybe she could get Ross to give her a ride on his horse. He had offered several times, but she had always turned him down.

WHEN SHE GOT to school early the next day, she looked all over for Ross but couldn't find him. Clay was doing rope tricks for a good-sized crowd of high school kids. Bonita watched as he twirled the lasso around himself and demonstrated his prowess at roping objects near and far. Blythe greeted her.

"Clay's really good. You should have seen what he did before you got here. He roped Wayne Manos when he was running away. I could watch him all day."

As she looked at Blythe's shining eyes, Bonita realized Blythe was infatuated with Clay. She giggled and elbowed her cousin.

"Blythe's got a feller!"

Blythe pushed her away. "So, what if I do? You think you're the only one the boys like? Me and Clay talk all the time."

She pushed back. "Don't be so touchy! I was just teasin' you a little."

Blythe's face blazed, and she put her outrage on public display.

"Stay away from me, Bonita McKindle! You think you're so pretty and so smart, and all you are is poor white trash!"

The crowd's attention was now on the two girls. Clay put his rope down and gawked at them. One of the older boys started yelling, "Fight! Fight!" and soon they were all yelling it.

Bonita ran away, in tears, completely mortified. She would go back home. At least there, no one called her names.

ON THE WAY home, she met Ross riding up on his horse. "You wanna play hooky with me today?'

"Sure, why not? That's what poor white trash does."

He dismounted and brought her close. "What's wrong, honey? Come here and let me hug you."

Resting in Ross's arms, Bonita told him what Blythe had done.

He patted her and wiped her tears away with his slightly soiled handkerchief. "Blythe had no call to talk to you like that! She's just jealous cause she's not pretty like you. Now let's just forget about her and school and have a good time."

"All right. But, first, do you have anything to eat? There wasn't nothin' to eat at my house this mornin'."

"Sure, I do. My ma fixes such a big breakfast that it keeps everybody full for hours, except for Clay, but he always eats like a horse. You can ride behind me, and I'll take you to a pretty spot, and you can eat my lunch like a picnic."

A FEW MINUTES later, she was sitting on the creek bank, gobbling down three biscuits filled with fresh ham and a fried pie filled with cinnamon spiced apples.

"This is so good, Ross. You're so lucky to have such a nice mother!"

Ross put down the cane fishing pole he had been whittling.

"Ma's almost always nice to me, but not so nice to Clay and Susan. I seen her beat Clay until the blood ran down his legs, but that was a while back. But Susan, she slapped the fire out of Susan a couple of days ago."

"That's hard to believe. Why did she slap Susan?"

"She found out Susan's goin' to have a baby."

"By Tommy Swimmer?"

"Yeah. Ma's mad because she wanted Susan to finish college and become a teacher."

Bonita laughed.

"What's so funny?"

"I wish I had your ma. My grandma told me once to not get uppity and think I could go to college and be a teacher. She thinks I should find a good man and get married."

"Well, maybe you should listen to her."

"Why do you say that?"

"It just seems to me that smart people ain't that happy. My ma is the smartest person I know, but she is miserable most of the time. Once in a while, Pa or Uncle John can get her to laughin', but before you know it, she's all upset again. It's hard on the whole family, especially Pa."

"Well, I still say I would love to have a mother who would see to it I don't go hungry and would push me to do my best in life."

"Believe me, it ain't that easy."

"It's a lot worse to have nobody but drunks livin' in your house."

"Maybe that will change someday."

"I sure hope so. Now, would you show me how to make my own fishin' pole?"

They spent the entire day together. They caught six fish between them, four catfish and two good-sized perch. After they roasted them over the fire they built, they sat by the fire and cuddled. Ross nibbled on Bonita's neck and chuckled.

She shivered. "That tickles. What are you laughin' at?"

"Just a picture I had in my mind."

She ran her fingers through his thick black hair. "Tell me about it."

"I was thinkin' about me and you, skinny dippin'."

"You devil! Know what? I need you to take me to your grandpa's store so I can get groceries."

"All right." He pulled her to her feet and pressed his body close to hers.

Feeling his manhood pulsating against her, she pushed him away. "Ross, we're not kids anymore, and we need to be careful."

"Don't worry, Bonita. I won't treat you like Tommy Swimmer treated my sister."

VII
FATEFUL
DECISIONS

PA AND SID eventually came back home, but two weeks later, Bonita woke up once again to a sink full of dirty dishes and vomit and worse in the floor. She decided she wasn't coming home to clean up another mess. Bonita had passed two birthdays, unnoticed, in her father's house. Now, she was fourteen. She stayed away every chance she got and would go home with any girl who would ask her.

She had once seen Martha Stone hold her nose when the Freedles left the store and remark to all who were standing by, "Trash! Poor white trash!"

She had never cared for Martha Stone and thought she was being her usual mean self. After all, only the Cherokees weren't white, and everybody in their community was poor, but that didn't mean they were trash. Ramona Freedle was a gentle, friendly girl, who had always admired her. Ramona looked dirty and had a powerful body odor, but Bonita knew that, in time, she could convince Ramona of the necessity of cleanliness.

She wasn't really planning on going home with Ramona because she didn't like the looks of her rough, burly brothers, but Sid's words to her that afternoon, when he came by the school, changed her mind.

"Sis, I know the house was a mess when you left, but you should've seen the old man today. He was so drunk he didn't know where he was at. Thought the whole house was the outhouse."

"Well, I'm not cleanin' it up! Let him clean up after hisself for once! Come on, Ramona, I'll go home with you after all."

Blythe saw what was happening and tried to intervene. "Mama and Daddy said you shouldn't be friendly with them Freedles. You might get in trouble if you go home with them."

"I don't care what Aunt Esther and Uncle Wade say. I'm old enough to take care of myself."

At this last remark, Ramona beamed, grabbed Bonita's arm, and propelled her down the road.

Bonita pulled away from Ramona, stopped, and turned to see Blythe walk away, crying. She knew her blabbermouth cousin would run home and tell her parents what had happened. Oh, well, even if they told Pa, he was so drunk he wouldn't even understand or care she was gone anyway. Lengthening her stride, she hurried to catch up with Ramona.

RAMONA CHATTERED HAPPILY to Bonita all the way to her house. "You're the first girl who's ever come home with me, and Pa told me I can bring anybody at any time." After a five-mile walk, mostly down a dirt road, they arrived at Ramona's home.

She had never seen a worse looking house in her life. The roof was sagging, the front porch had several boards missing, and most of the windows were boarded up. Even the bone-thin dogs, who seemed too lazy or too hungry to bark or even wag their tails, reflected neglect.

They didn't seem to hear when Ramona said, "Git out of here, you mangy ol' dogs!"

Her brothers kicked them, hard, and they yelped with pain and shuffled off into the woods behind the shack.

"Come on in, girls! Who's your purty young friend, 'Mona?" A toothless, foul-smelling old man draped a sweaty arm around Bonita's shoulders and gave her an unwelcome squeeze.

"This here is Bonita McKindle, and don't you be botherin' her!" Ramona removed her from the smelly embrace.

"Don't be so unfriendly, sister. Yeah, I know you, gal. You're Anderson's girl, ain't you?"

"Yes, I am."

"Well, now I've knowed your father for nigh on thirty years. We've swigged many a bottle a'tween us, and that's a fact."

"We gotta go and help Ma with supper, Pa."

Ma was a sullen, dried-up little woman, who seemed as silent as her husband was talkative. She barely grunted when Ramona introduced her to Bonita. She handed the girls some potatoes to peel while she fed a small baby a bottle of milk. She lay the baby down in a big wooden box by the cook stove and tended to something smoldering in a huge, rusty pot.

AFTER THE GIRLS peeled the potatoes, they took a walk in the woods while supper was being cooked. Ma had sent the boys to gather some more firewood for the wood stove.

"At least your brothers tend to the chores, unlike my lazy brother."

"Yeah, I guess when they ain't fightin' or drinkin' moonshine."

"Come here, Ramona, let me French braid your hair for you." She gently pushed the girl down on a big rock, took bobby pins and a brush and comb from her purse, and began the painstaking process of bringing Ramona's thick locks under control.

"Ow! That hurts!"

"Well, I got to get the rats out first. How long has it been since you gave your hair a good brushin'?"

"I don't know. I ain't never got time for stuff like that."

"Well, you gotta take the time. I brush my hair out ever mornin' and night. See how it shines?"

"You got real purty hair, all right. But mine won't never look like yours."

"Something else I do. I wash my hair two or three times a week, and I always put vinegar in my final rinse. That helps with the shine."

"Two or three times a week! Say, how often do you bathe?"

"Except for the wintertime, I bathe every day. In the winter, it's kinda hard to heat up enough water, and the days are so short and dark, but I try to bathe every other day."

"All that bathin' weakens a body. Least that's what Pa always says. Ain't you sick an awful lot?"

"Me? I'm as healthy as a horse."

"That's right strange."

"You know, Ramona, if you would fix your hair and take a bath, you would be real pretty."

"Do you really think so?"

"I know so. Look at yourself." Bonita handed Ramona her compact.

"I don't look half bad at that."

"I'll say. You got those sparkly green eyes, and I love the color of your hair, kinda blondish brown. Let me put a little lipstick and rouge on you."

"Where do you get all this stuff?"

"I charge it at the Stones."

"Don't your pa get mad?"

"Sure. He rants and rages every month, but then he pays it, goes and gets drunk, and forgets all about it until the next month."

Ramona slowly returned the mirror. She looked down at the ground and started to tremble. "Does your pa do bad things when he's drunk?"

"Sure, he does! He drinks up his whole check every month, and sometimes he pukes and takes dumps all over the house, and he brings his old drinkin' cronies home for me to cook for and wait on."

"But does he ever, you know, bother you?"

"What do you mean by bother?"

"You know. Does he ever touch you in a bad way?"

She began to understand. "No, never. Does your pa force you?"

"Yes!"

Rocking on her heels, holding her stomach, Ramona cried uncontrollably. All Bonita could think to do was pat her shoulder.

Finally, she thought of something to say. "Have you told your ma?"

"She don't believe me."

"How about your brothers?"

Ramona lifted her glazed, pained eyes up to Bonita. "If they catch me out by myself, they try to do the same thing. Did you see that baby Ma was feedin' when we come in?"

"Yes."

"That's my baby, and I don't even know which one the pa is."

"Oh, Ramona! Don't your ma know then?"

"She tries to say it was a boy at school. But you know the boys at school don't come near me, lookin' the way I look." At this, Ramona began wiping the makeup from her face and tore the bobby pins from her hair. "I can't look nice around anyone. You understand, don't you?"

"I understand. But, Ramona, you gotta get away from this place!"

"I know that, and I'm tryin'. Let me show you somethin'."

Ramona led her to an old oak tree. She reached her hand into a hollow place and pulled out a small tin box. "See here? I got quite a bit saved up."

She knelt, spread her dress before her, and poured the money out upon it. "I got nearly thirty dollars here. When I get fifty, I'm goin' to walk to Tahlequah and buy me a bus ticket out of this place. I'll get me a job in a big city somewhere and never come back. I need fifty so's I have somethin' to live on until I can get a job. You're probably wonderin' where I got this kind of money, ain't you? Well, some of it I earned by selling walnuts and pop bottles, and some of it I stole. Does that make you hate me?"

"Of course not! If I was in your shoes, I would do anything I could to get out. But how about your baby?"

"Well, the way I figure it, he's not really mine since I never asked for him. Ma will take care of him, and he's a boy so they won't bother him."

"How do you keep from gettin' another one?"

"I run fast, I have a lot of hidin' places, and I don't take no chances. I wouldn't have got no baby if it hadn't been for me bein' sick last winter. One day they caught Ma at town, and me in bed so sick I couldn't even lift my head. That's when I got him, but it won't happen again. You know this money feels damp. Maybe I better move it somewhere inside."

She pulled out a dirty handkerchief from her pocket, placed the coins and currency in it, and tied the ends of the handkerchief together. She then placed the homemade bag in her bra.

"Wait a minute. I got a dollar I got out of Pa's overalls when he was asleep. Take it."

"Thanks, Bonita. I don't get dollars very often." She rolled it up carefully and put it in her bra.

THEY RETURNED TO the house to see the boys had almost devoured all the food from the table. Bonita sat down between Ramona and her mother, not wanting to get close to the boys, who were gobbling, barely chewing their food before swallowing, and smacking loudly. Even Anderson and his drunken friends had better table manners. They reminded her of starved hounds.

Bellowing like a mad bull, Freedle confronted his sons. "You boys, leave off now and let these girls have somethin' to eat!"

The tallest boy glared at him. "But I'm still hungry, Pa. Girls don't do nothin' to need to eat no how."

"I said leave off!" He raised his knife to the face of the offending son.

The brothers hastily left the table, muttering obscenities under their breaths.

Bonita's stomach was growling. Pa grinned at her and lifted the lid off the big pot Ma had been stirring. "Have some fresh stewed possum, girls."

It took all her self-control to take a small piece of the offered meat on her plate and eat it. Possums ate dead things. Squirrel, rabbit, and deer were fine when cooked properly. But possum! She mixed the meat in with the fried potatoes and beans so that she couldn't taste it as well. She finally choked a small serving down. Ramona ate hers like it was fried chicken.

"No wonder you're so skinny, girl. You don't eat enough to keep a bird alive. Don't you want some more?"

"No thank you. I'm not very hungry."

"Suit yourself."

They avoided the front room where the males gathered around the rusty pot belly stove to swig from a jug and talk. They kept busy with clearing the table and washing the dishes. After they finished, Bonita grabbed a worn-out broom and began to sweep the dirty kitchen floor.

Ma grabbed the broom out of her hands. "No need to do that. It's too dark to see anyway. Feed your baby brother, Mona."

Ramona sat at the kitchen table and gave the baby a bottle of milk. Her mother had previously fed him gravy while they were eating supper.

Bonita sat beside Ramona and watched. Ramona held the baby as far away as she could. She didn't cuddle him the way her mother had. The baby looked healthy and a lot like his mother.

When Ramona had finished feeding the baby, she changed his wet diaper, and handed him back to her mother.

Bonita realized she had never heard the baby make a sound.

"He sure don't cry much."

Ma kissed the baby's chubby cheeks. "No, little Otto is a real good baby. No trouble a'tall." She put the baby back in the large wooden box.

"Come on, Bonita. Let's go to bed."

Pa stood up and gestured to them. "Goin' to bed so soon, girls? Why don't you come and set a spell with us?"

"We're tired, Pa, and we got to go to school tomorrow."

The shorter brother smirked. "That's what you always say."

"Well, it's always true."

RAMONA LED HER to a small narrow bed in the corner of her parents' room. It had sheets hanging around it for a little privacy. After changing into a flannel gown that Ramona gave her, Bonita lay down between the dirty, stained sheets.

"I'm sorry we're so crowded, but I usually sleep by myself."

"Do you think anybody will bother us?"

"I don't think so, with us being in the same room with Ma and all. No one's ever touched me in this room. When I was little, I used to have to sleep with my brothers in the boys' room. That was all right until they got big. I begged Ma for a bed of my own, and she finally told Pa to get me one. He found this one in the junkyard a couple of years ago, and I've been sleepin' here ever since. Don't worry, you'll be all right."

But sometime early in the morning, Bonita awoke to a sickening odor above her. She looked up to see Ramona's father looking down at them. She quickly shook Ramona awake.

"Ramona, it's your pa."

Ramona spoke quietly, "Go on to bed, Pa, or I'll scream and wake Ma up. It's all right, Bonita. He does that sometimes, but nothing comes of it."

But Freedle didn't leave.

NEITHER BONITA, RAMONA, nor the Freedle brothers were at school the next morning. As soon as Blythe noticed their absence, she ran home.

"Daddy, remember me tellin' you that Bonita went home with the Freedles yesterday? She wasn't at school this morning, and neither was the Freedles!"

Esther came in from hanging clothes on the line. "Blythe, what are you doin' home?"

After repeating her story to her mother, Blythe asked, "What are we gonna do?"

"Your daddy is goin' right over to see Anderson and tell him about Bonita. He's probably so drunk he don't know she's missin'. If that don't work, we will go to the sheriff."

Wade stomped on a cigarette butt he had thrown to the ground. "You know how the McKindles feel about the law. I would druther not get them mixed up in this."

"We'll do what is necessary. No tellin' what those dirty Freedles have done to that child! I know you think you're tough, but you better take your gun and get Anderson to take his, too, if he's sober enough to shoot it."

IT TOOK WADE'S throwing several pans of water in Anderson's face before he sobered up enough to listen.

"You mean the Freedles have Bonita? Well, now, I'm not too worried. Old man Freedle and me have been friends for a long time. He wouldn't hurt my girl."

"Anderson, ain't you heard the tales on the Freedles? That old man was arrested for tryin' to sell a neighbor woman for a whore!"

"Freedle told me the woman was willin', and she just cried rape when she saw her husband drivin' up."

"That's not the way I heard it. Now, are you goin' with me to the Freedles, or do I need to get the law?"

"No need of that. I'll go with you."

"Take your shotgun."

"I will, but I won't need it. This is just some kind of misunderstandin', and that's all."

AN HOUR LATER, they found themselves in front of a filthy,

dilapidated house. A couple of mangy dogs got up, looked at them disinterestedly, and then lay back down.

"Lord, have mercy, Anderson! You would let your girl come to a place like this?"

"I hardly ever know where she is. She never tells me nothin'."

"Maybe she does, and you're just too drunk to listen."

Anderson flushed red and dropped his eyes. "Yeah, maybe so."

Wade banged on the door, but no one answered. "It's probably locked. Maybe I can kick it down."

The short, muscular Wade backed up, took a short run, and shattered the wooden door with one hard kick. "That was easy. Wood must be rotten." Reaching through the hole he made, he unlocked the door and swung it open."

As soon as they walked in, they heard a baby crying. In a small bedroom off the kitchen, they found an unkempt, unconscious woman, lying on a filthy mattress atop a rusty metal bed. Beside her was a wailing two or three-month-old infant, wearing a soiled diaper.

Wade wrinkled his nose and shook her. "Where's Bonita?"

She opened her matted eyes and looked at them. "Who's Bonita?"

"That's my niece. What did you Freedles do to her?"

She recovered her wits and sat up in the bed. "You must mean Mona's little friend. Pa said he was takin' all them kids to the Muskogee Fair today. I wanted to go, but he said I needed to take my medicine and rest. Guess he gave me a little too much from the looks of little Otto."

"Anderson, you stay with her. I am goin' to look around some more. Where did she sleep?"

"Her and Mona slept behind those sheets over there. "

Wade came back in a few minutes with something in his hand. "This is peculiar, Anderson."

"What's that?"

"That big, old, black purse that she always carries around is still here. She never goes anywhere without this purse, does she?"

Anderson leaned over until his face was a few inches from the woman's. "No, she don't. Lady, if your man or one of your boys hurt Bonita, I will kill whoever did it, dead."

She raised herself up and grabbed his arm. "Please don't, Mister McKindle. We would all starve to death if my husband is gone, and I don't want to lose one of my boys either. If you hurry, you can get her and bring her back, safe and sound."

"That's what we aim to do. Gimme her purse, Wade. Let's go."

TWO HOURS EARLIER Ramona Freedle had been pleading with her father, as they drove toward Muskogee.

"Come on, Pa. You gotta let Bonita out of the trunk. She might suffocate back there!"

"Don't worry, Mona. She's passed out like your ma and doesn't even know where she is. Besides that old turtle hull has so many holes in it that it has plenty of air. They'll get her out when we get to Muskogee."

"Why are you doin' this to her? It was bad enough when you did it to me, but you have no right to do it to Bonita!"

"A man's gotta do what a man's gotta do to keep his family fed. Your low-class carcass got us one hundred dollars, and we are almost out of money to buy food and gas. Bonita's going to make us two hundred dollars. She won't be hurt, just diddled a little, and we'll come get her tomorrow. Next thing she knows she's wakin' up in her own front yard."

A series of loud thuds came from the back of the car.

Ramona's tall brother said, "Think she's awake, Pa."

Freedle cursed. "I must not have give her enough."

"She's awake all right! And what's goin' to keep her from turnin' you in to the law?"

"She's Anderson McKindle's daughter, so no one's goin' believe her. Besides, she was knocked out and blindfolded when we loaded her in the trunk. Mona, if you will just keep your big mouth shut, there's no way she can identify us. She's gonna stay with my friends in Muskogee all day and all night, and while she's there, we are going to the law ourselves to report her missin'. We can say we was out lookin' for her was why we waited a bit before we reported her missin'. Believe me I thought of ever'thing! But if this scheme's gonna work, they'll have to knock her out again. She can't get loose or get her blindfold off, but I sure thought she would stay asleep longer. We're halfway to Fort Gibson, so we will be at Muskogee in a few minutes. You kids stay in the car when we get there. I'll run in, tell them about the problem, and let them deal with it. Then I'll get the money, and we'll be on our way."

Ramona made herself smile. "Well, Pa. I have to say that this time you really thought of ever'thing. It will be nice to get somethin' to eat besides wild game."

"Thanks, Mona. I'm glad you finally figured out how smart your old man is." He gave Ramona's knee an appreciative squeeze.

When the Freedles were about five miles from Ft. Gibson, an ominous thumping sound started coming from the left front tire.

Freedle screamed a stream of obscenities. "We got a flat, and we got to fix it! We'll have to get the tire out of the trunk without lettin' the girl know it's us. Ever'body, just keep your mouths shut."

Freedle steered the car off the highway onto a dirt road. When they opened the trunk, Bonita was squirming and kicking with all of her strength, but she was still tightly bound, blindfolded, and gagged. Pa motioned for Ramona to throw her body over Bonita to restrain her while the boys got the heavy tire out of the trunk.

Ramona did what he said, but while they were busy with the tire, she untied Bonita's hands and feet and took off the blindfold and gag. She helped Bonita out of the trunk.

"Run!"

The girls sped off into the nearby woods.

UNFORTUNATELY, THEY WERE spotted and were soon pursued by two fast runners.

"Run for the road, Bonita! I can slow these two down. Pa can't run worth a lick so just stay out of his reach."

"I'll send help for you!" Bonita ran off.

RAMONA PICKED UP a large tree branch and whacked her brothers with it. By the time they got it away from her, she saw Bonita had almost reached the highway. As the boys took turns smashing their fists into her face and body, she knew she was going to die.

From a distance, Ramona heard her pa yell, "Stop!"

She looked up and saw him glaring down at her. "My turn, boys."

Pa threw several vicious punches on the side of her head. "Leave her lay there! Stupid girl ruined a good tire by pokin' holes in it, and even worse, she may have cost me two hundred dollars today, so, I don't care if she lives or dies. If anyone asks me about her, I'll just say that she disappeared with Bonita. Let's change the flat and find that hussy. She can't have got far."

Her vision failed, and she felt herself drifting away.

NOT HESITATING, BONITA kept running in the direction of Tahlequah. She considered stopping to ask for help at a nearby house, but she heard some barking dogs, so she kept running. What she needed was a place to hide and catch her breath. It would take the Freedles time to change their flat and come after her. Spotting an old barn on the other side of the highway, she crossed over to check it out. It had a loft in it where she could hide and get a good view of anyone approaching. The wooden ladder was rickety but strong enough to hold her light weight, so she climbed it and positioned herself where she could see.

After she felt rested, Bonita thought about running some more but reasoned the Freedles might see her from the road and catch her again. She decided to stay where she was and keep watch. Her sharp eyes caught sight of the Freedles driving slowly down the highway toward Tahlequah. The two huge boys had their heads hanging out the windows, looking on both sides of the road for her. They made her think of dogs again. This time they were dogs who were going for a ride in the family car. Where was Ramona? She probably had gotten away from them. If the Freedles didn't come back and find her in the barn, she would wait until dark and walk back toward Tahlequah. Uncle Arthur's oldest son lived on the outskirts of Tahlequah, and he would help her.

Bonita watched for some time, once almost running out to flag down one of the few vehicles she saw on the road. She didn't because she was afraid she would choose the wrong car. Some bad people, like the Freedles, might be in it. Out of the corner of her eye, she glimpsed a familiar blue pickup.

It was Uncle Wade! The fear she had been fighting melted away. Standing in the barn's loft opening, she waved her arms and yelled. But it was no good. They would never see or hear her.

Scrambling down the ladder, she ran to the edge of the field but stopped in her tracks when she saw the Freedles' car on the road again. Now they were heading toward Ft. Gibson. Uncle Wade must have seen them in his rear-view mirror because he suddenly pulled off the highway and then back on to the highway, directly behind the Freedles. He honked his horn and rammed the back of the old jalopy. Freedle pulled off the road to get away from the crazy driver, only to find himself and his sons confronted by Uncle Wade and her pa, both packing shotguns.

JUDGING HERSELF TO be safe, Bonita ran down the highway to where the two vehicles were parked, yelling, "I'm here!" She ran as fast as she could and grabbed her father's shoulder when she reached him. "Pa, I'm so glad you came for me!"

Freedle was trying to talk his way out of trouble. "Anderson, I thought we was friends! Why, I would never hurt your little girl! I was just takin' them to the fair, but your girl had some kind of spell."

"Then why did you drug me, tie me up, and throw me in the trunk of your car?"

"You don't remember that fit you had? Why, you was foamin' at the mouth, sayin' all kinds of crazy things! We tied you up to keep you from hurtin' us or yourself, and we was takin' you to the doctor."

"I don't believe you. Ramona helped me escape. Where is she now?"

"See, that there shows you are out of your head! Ramona never come with us."

"Pa, don't believe him! If you will just drive a little ways down the road, I will show you where I last saw Ramona."

"Wade, you stay here and watch these varmints. Bonita and me will take a little ride."

BONITA TOOK HIM to the place where she escaped.

"Ramona, where are you?"

They heard a moan and saw Ramona, bleeding freely from where she had been hit about her face and head, walking slowly toward them.

Anderson shook his head in disbelief. "Did that no-good do that to you, girl?"

Ramona nodded and fell into Bonita's arms.

"Oh, Ramona, you saved me! I will always thank you for that!"

Anderson took off his outer shirt and tore his undershirt into strips. "Put these around her head and face to stop the bleedin'. Come on, girl, you can stay with us as long as you need to."

WHEN THEY GOT back to where Wade and the Freedles were, Anderson exploded.

"You lyin' dog!" He hauled off and slammed his big fist into the side of Freedle's jaw.

Freedle fell to the ground and begged. "Don't kill me, Anderson! My family will starve to death without me! "

"I oughta kill you and these worthless whelps! But you got a poor woman and a mite at home. I will spare you for their sake, but if you or any of your kind come near either of these girls again, I will shoot you down like the mad dog you are! Come on girls. Let's get you home."

Before they left, Bonita turned to Wade and hugged him. "Thank you, Uncle Wade. I will never forget what you did for me today."

Wade's dark eyes filled with tears. "And I will never forget the promise I made your ma the night she died. I promised her I would always watch after her children."

Anderson wiped his eyes. "Thank God you keep your promises better than I do."

AFTER RAMONA WAS feeling well enough to talk, she told them she had used a knife to make small, unnoticeable holes in the front tire. She hoped they would have a flat before they got to Muskogee, which they did.

Anderson praised Ramona for being so smart and thanked her for saving Bonita.

Bonita was overjoyed to have a girl her age live with them. Ramona did more than her share of chores, and she began to take an interest in her appearance. Bonita didn't have to tell her to clean up and make herself look nice. Now, Ramona did it with pleasure.

ONE MORNING, BONITA overheard Mr. Stone, who was

a blacksmith as well as a storekeeper, remark he could use some help with keeping the stables clean.

"My grandsons used to do it for me for spending money, but their pa and Uncle John keep them pretty busy with chores around their places these days. I usually only see them some Saturdays, and then they only have time to help around the store. Wish't I knew of some strong young'un who needed the work and the money."

Bonita immediately thought of Ramona. "Mister Stone, I know Ramona Freedle would be glad to do it for you."

"A girl? No, I don't think so. Muckin' out a filthy stable would be too much for a girl."

"But, Mister Stone, Ramona is as strong as a mule, and she really needs the money. She wouldn't mind the mess, and I know she would work cheap."

At this last remark, Martha's eyes lit up. "Go ahead and try her, Josh. Bein' a Freedle she won't mind the stink and won't expect you to pay her an arm and a leg like most."

That was how Ramona found a job, cleaning up after horses every weekend for fifty cents. One day she bragged to Bonita, "I'm sure glad that I put that money in my bra before Pa drug us to Fort Gibson. With what I saved and what I've earned, I got sixty dollars."

"Well, since you don't have to run off anymore, we'll just have to go on a shoppin' trip sometime."

AS FOR ANDERSON, he was a changed man. He didn't drink, and he began to take an interest in Bonita, treating her the way a father should. His drinking buddies soon learned they were no longer welcome in Anderson's home.

Bonita and Ramona got up in a clean house every morning, ate a nourishing breakfast that they took turns cooking, and packed themselves a hearty meal in their lunch buckets. They went off to school, ready to learn and have fun with their friends.

Along in the spring, a stomach ailment swept through the school, almost emptying the classrooms. Ramona fell victim to it, but Bonita remained healthy.

Anderson insisted she attend school by herself. "I ain't completely helpless with sickness, you know. I can stir up a pot of soup for Mona when she feels like eatin' again. You go on to school, and I'll stay home and watch after her."

As she approached the rock school building, Bonita looked all around, but the place appeared deserted. It wasn't until she went inside that she stumbled upon Clay and his sister Emily, sitting on a wooden bench in front of the principal's office.

"Where is everybody?"

"Home sick with the flu I suppose. There's where Ross, Mary, and Zack are. They told us to wait here until enough kids show up to have a class. Most of the teachers were too sick to report to work today so the principal is teaching whatever high school age kids show up. The two or three healthy teachers that are here today are teaching the lower grades."

Bonita giggled. "You know I think that is the most you have ever said to me."

As Clay blushed and quit talking, Emily spoke up. "He can talk when he wants to. It's just that when Ross is around, no one else can get a word in edgewise." She stopped talking and pointed. "Oh, look, here come the Adairs."

Bonita spent the next hour talking and laughing with Emily, Clay, and the other students who straggled in. It was the first time she had really talked to Emily, who was two years ahead of her in school. Emily was not as pretty as her older sister, Susan, having straight, dark brown hair, which she wore in a braided bun, and plain features. Her dark brown eyes were large and framed by long lashes but were hard to see behind the thick glasses she wore. Bonita had heard Emily described as smart and sweet, but no one had mentioned Emily's sense of humor or her love of funny tales.

Since Ross wasn't present to defend himself, she kept everyone laughing with stories about him. "Clay, remember when Ross got the idea he could build his own airplane?"

Clay grinned. "I remember, but I think it was more of a glider."

"Maybe so. Anyway, it was about this long and this wide." Emily used her hands to indicate the glider's dimensions. "He worked on it a long time to get it big enough to hold him. He waited until Pa was gone, and Ma was busy working in the house to test it out. Of course, we kids were all watching him. He climbed up to the highest point on the roof, which was pretty high since we live in a two-story house, and strapped himself in. Then he started running, and when he got to the edge of the roof, he jumped off. Next thing we knew, Ross and his contraption hit the ground, and it shattered into a hundred pieces!"

Bonita's eyes got big. "Was he hurt?"

"Just his ears from Ma scolding him."

Clay rolled his eyes. "Yeah, if it had been me, my rear end would have been sore for a week from the whuppin' Ma gave me."

Principal Maxwell came out of his office at the end of the hour. "Good! There are ten of you now, and that's enough to have class."

Bonita discovered, not only was their principal knowledgeable in several academic areas, he was a gifted teacher. He drew out the most reticent of students by asking them questions about subjects which interested them. She had suspected that quiet Clay was smart, but he seldom spoke up in class. Maxwell looked straight at Clay and asked, "Can anyone tell me which side the Cherokees supported during the Civil War?"

Clay spent the next several minutes, explaining how and why the Cherokees were divided during the war. Their principal smiled and encouraged him by asking questions, all of which Clay answered with apparent ease.

After they were dismissed, Emily teased him. "And here I thought I was going to be the teacher of the family. Looks like my little brother is going to give me a run for my money."

Clay scoffed. "Me, be a teacher? You know better. I couldn't stand bein' cooped up with a bunch of silly kids all day. Come on, let's eat. I'm hungry."

Emily linked arms with Bonita. "When aren't you hungry, Clay?"

Bonita sat between Clay and Emily at lunch and was surprised when Clay offered her a fried peach pie. "Did your ma make them? If she did, please give me one. Ross gave me an apple one she made once, and I can still remember how good it tasted. "

Emily poked Clay in the side. "How come you got two pies in your lunch bucket?"

"Well, Ross didn't feel like eating his, so I took it so it wouldn't go to waste."

She poked him again. "No, for sure, we wouldn't want that to happen. Why didn't you offer it to your favorite sister?"

"I thought Bonita might appreciate it more, and she did."

"I sure did. Thanks, Clay."

Emily tapped her forehead. "All right. I'll remember that next time you ask me to let you in the window when you miss your curfew."

After school was out, Bonita was surprised to see Clay standing on the front steps. "You want a ride home, Bonita?"

"Sure, if it's not too much trouble."

"No trouble at all. Here, let me help you up. Old Tall Boy lives up to his name."

"He sure does! What kind of horse is he?"

"He's part Percheron. They make good draft horses. Real handy to have around a farm, too. We use him to break the garden every spring, and he's gentle as a lamb for ridin'."

She stood on tiptoes to pat the horse's nose. "I can tell he's a good boy. Shouldn't we wait for Emily?"

"Nah, she's too busy talkin' to Mark Adair. She'll ride home when she feels like it."

CLAY TOOK A long, winding route to Bonita's house. He

stopped once and pointed to a nearby bluff. "See that cave over there? That's where the McKindles used to have a still. The revenuers caught them makin' whiskey there one night, busted up the still, and threw the two that was there in jail."

"I'm sure they was kin to me."

"Yeah, I believe so. Your grandpa, George McKindle, and his brother, Bert."

"I guess that's why some people look down their noses at me and Pa."

"Don't let them bother you. They likely have someone in their family who's just as bad or worse."

Tall Boy abruptly stopped his easy trot with a nervous nicker, showing the whites of his eyes.

Clay stroked his forelock and spoke comforting words. "Easy, boy. What spooked you?"

Bonita gasped and clutched his arm. "Clay, there's a man, standin' in the shadows watchin' us."

He signaled for Tall Boy to turn so he could see who Bonita was talking about. Bonita felt his body stiffen as he called out, "Hello, sir. We're just passin' through now, and we'll be on our way."

Bonita didn't recognize the gravelly voice that responded. "See that you do, boy. You better leave now and take that pretty little gal with you, if want to keep her, and you both better forget you ever seen me."

Clay jerked on the reins and wheeled away. "Come on, Tall Boy. Let's go."

In a few minutes, Tall Boy's easy lope switched to a quick canter. Bonita clung to Clay's waist and hid her tearful face in his broad back. They didn't speak until he stopped the horse about a mile from her house.

"Who was that, Clay?"

"Just another bootlegger. 'Course it could be Machine Gun Kelly or some other outlaw. People are always sayin' they like to hide out around here." He turned his head and saw her tear stained face. "It's all right, Bonita. You're safe now. Here, take my hanky."

Bonita wiped her face and took several deep breaths to calm herself. "What would have happened if that man had been on a horse? He might have caught us and killed us!"

"Let me help you down, and I'll tell you somethin'."

After Clay helped Bonita down, he kept his arms around her for several minutes. "Bonita, if it had come down to a fight, I would have jumped off Tall Boy and sent you on your way. Then I would have pulled out my knife and given Mr. Mystery Man the fight of his life."

"What if he had a gun?"

"Well, I would have dealt with it the best I could, but whatever happened, I would have kept you safe." He pulled her close to him and gave her a long, passionate kiss.

In the middle of the kiss, Bonita thought about Ross and tried to push him away. It was like trying to push a mountain.

He finished the kiss, stepped back, and stared at her. "Now, can you honestly tell me you didn't like that just like I did?"

She glared at him. "Yes, I'll admit it. I liked it, but that don't make it right. I have a boyfriend— Ross— and I shouldn't be kissin' around with his brother."

He chuckled. "All right, Bonita. I can wait. You'll get tired of Ross one of these days. Guess I'll go to Tahlequah on Monday and tell the sheriff what we saw today."

Bonita grabbed his shoulders. "Please don't do that!"

He turned his head to face her. "Why not? The law needs to know so he can run him off or arrest him."

"Somethin' bad might be goin' on in them woods, and I don't want you or me hurt. And maybe we better keep what happened between us just in case. Promise me you won't tell."

"All right, but you need to promise me you'll never come by these woods again."

"Don't worry about that. I won't. Thanks for the ride, but could you take me home now? I need to see about Ramona."

RAMONA RAISED UP from her sick bed when she saw Bonita's ashen face. "What's wrong?"

"I ain't supposed to tell."

"Maybe not, but you will tell me."

After Bonita recited what had happened in the woods, Ramona panicked. "You could have been killed! Tell your pa right now."

But when she told her father about her harrowing experience, he laughed at her. "All you had to do was tell that man who you are. When he heard you was Anderson McKindle's daughter, he would have let you alone."

Her temper flared. "And what if he didn't know who Anderson McKindle was? What then?"

"Not much chance of that. If he didn't know me, he would have at least known the McKindle name. My pa was on good terms with the James brothers, Belle Starr, and the rest. Pretty Boy Floyd was a good friend of mine until the law killed him. As for Kelly, I know him and lots of others. You was never in any real danger. 'Course I can't say the same for the Stone boy, but most likely, unless he lost his head and done somethin' foolish, he wouldn't be hurt either. Now tell me, what did this here scary man look like?"

"He was standin' in the shadows, so we never seen his face. All I could tell was he didn't look as big as Clay, and he had a rough soundin' voice."

"That description could fit several I know."

"Should we tell the sheriff?"

"'Course not. When did the law ever do anything for us, except kill our people and our friends? No, best not to tell nobody else. That way nobody will get throwed in jail or hurt."

Lives were changed forever because Bonita listened to her father and told no one.

MINERVA PETTIBONE'S STYLISH appearance was the

envy of Bonita, Ramona, and the other girls at Jubilee High School. She had transferred from an elite Tulsa high school at the insistence of her divorcée mother, who left Minerva with her aunt at Jubilee while she took an extended European vacation with her new husband. When the females of Jubilee High first glimpsed Minerva's slender form, arrayed in a tailored floral dress, with a matching hat and handbag, shod with gleaming white patent leather shoes, they were overcome with feelings of inadequacy.

Girls and boys alike were asking, "Who's that girl?"

Minerva didn't belong in a small community school, and she wasn't shy about letting her fellow students know it, if they were in earshot of her conversation with her few select friends. "It's only a temporary arrangement. Mother said she will be back in May to take me home. Then she'll buy me a Ford Roadster, and I will be back with my school chums in the fall."

Minerva and her small circle of friends sat at their own table before school and during lunch. Minerva complained loudly about "having to eat outside like farmers," as she waited for one of her companions to arrange the tablecloth and dinnerware she brought with her to school each day.

One day, Bonita ventured close enough to see what the group was eating. She ran back to where Blythe, Ramona, Ross, and Clay were sitting. "Looks like Queen Minerva is serving lunch meat sandwiches with some kind of cheese, soda pop, and Baby Ruth candy bars."

Ross snickered. "Shoot, Bonita! I could have told you most of that. The meat, light bread, cheese, soda pop, and candy all comes from Grandpa's store. Minerva's aunt comes every Saturday to stock up for the following week, and Grandma falls all over herself to wait on her."

"Does the Queen ever come to the store?"

"Just seen her there a couple of times when her and her friends rode their bikes over to get a soda pop. 'Course she didn't know any of us, and I quit tryin' to speak to her when she snubbed me the first time. Think she actually spoke to Clay once, didn't she?"

"Well, she's in my grade so we have classes together. All she said was, 'Nice show', when her group watched me do my ropin' at the store one day."

Blythe patted Clay on the cheek. "Hope you don't get to thinkin' you're too good to be seen with us."

He smirked. "Don't worry. I know my place, for now. Let's change the subject. Do you girls want to go ridin' with us tomorrow? Since it's Saturday, and the crops are all in, Pa said we could do what we want all day."

Under the table, Ross squeezed Bonita's knee. "Good idea! We can meet you girls at the store in the mornin', and me and Clay can show you some real pretty places."

Ramona, who hadn't said anything, spoke up, "I can't go. I'll be cleaning out your grandpa's stables in the mornin'."

Bonita frowned. "Can't you put it off until Sunday?"

"No, I promised I would do it tomorrow, and I like to keep my promises. Besides, remember we told your granny we would be at church on Sunday?"

"That's right. I almost forgot."

WHEN BONITA WAS brushing her hair out that night, she noticed Ramona's silence. "Mona, you sure have been quiet lately. Anything wrong?"

"Not really. I just get tired of being the odd one out."

"What do you mean by that?"

"You and Ross are a couple, and Blythe wants her and Clay to be a couple. I don't have nobody."

Putting down her brush, she turned to look back at Ramona. "And whose fault is that? You don't say five words to anybody but me at school."

"I can't help it. Ever' time someone looks at me, I wonder if they're seein' that bushy-headed, dirty girl I was last year."

"I think that's all in your imagination."

"I don't think so. Genevieve Murdock asked me the other day if I ever see my nasty brothers anymore."

"Well, not everybody feels that way. You have all of us as friends."

"Only because they're your friends."

She sat down on the bed beside Ramona and hugged her. "I wish there was somethin' I could do to make you feel better."

Ramona stood up and smiled down at her. "You've already changed my life, Bonita, and I will always be grateful for that. Now, you go off and have fun with your friends tomorrow. Don't worry about me. Someday I will go someplace where nobody knows me, and I will start my life all over again."

The next morning, after they were treated to soda pop and peanuts, Bonita and Blythe rode off with their beaus. Bonita looked over at Blythe and smiled when she saw her nervous expression. "Don't worry. Tall Boy is big, but he's really gentle."

Ross turned around with a puzzled look on his face. "How do you know he's named Tall Boy, and how do you know he's gentle?"

"Oh, Clay gave me a ride home last week when you was sick."

"Hmmm…why didn't you mention that to me, Clay?"

Clay shooed the fly away that was circling Tall Boy's head. "Didn't seem worth mentionin'. Where you wanna go first?"

"Let's take them to the swingin' bridge."

Bonita took in the beautiful view of the crystal-clear river below, snaking its way through the boulders and uprooted trees which were scattered throughout its path.

Blythe suddenly screamed and held on to Clay's arm as Ross jumped up and down on the swaying planks a few feet in front of them. "Make him stop, Clay! He's goin' to bounce us all off!"

Bonita tried to calm her. "Quit screamin', Blythe. Just hang on to the rope on both sides of the bridge, and you'll be all right."

Clay raised his voice. "Knock it off, Ross! You're scarin' the girls."

"Aww, ya'll are no fun! Come here, Bonita, and let me show you somethin' pretty." Ross grabbed her hand and pulled her to him. "See that limestone hill across the river there?"

"Uh-huh."

"Look right there on the side of the bluff. You see that shape?"

"I see somethin'. Looks like a bird."

"That's what it is, an eagle. That's part of the Wauhillau community. Did you know it means eagle in Cherokee? They say it was named that after Katie Eagle Goback, one of the early settlers."

"That's so pretty! How come you know so much about the Cherokees?"

Clay spoke up behind them. "Ross knows all about the Cherokees and even knows how to speak it. Grandpa Clay taught him how."

Blythe smiled brightly. "I'm half-Cherokee, too, you know. My daddy has a roll number, but he can't remember much of the language. Bonita's the only *u-ne-ga* here."

"What did you call me?"

"*U-ne-ga* It means white."

Bonita tossed her head. "Well, that shows what you know. Granny says she could have signed-up for the Dawes, but Grandpa wouldn't let her."

"Oh, I heard that old tale a hundred times, but it don't matter. If you or your parents didn't sign up on the roll, you ain't Cherokee."

Eyes flashing, she turned to confront Blythe. "I don't care what you or anybody else says! I'm part Cherokee, and I always will be!"

Ross swatted Bonita on the rear and guffawed. "Man, Clay! If I had known talkin' Cherokee would get Bonita this hot, I would have done it a long time ago."

She rounded on him with a quick slap. "I told you not to touch me there!"

Ross rubbed his jaw and grinned sheepishly. "Sorry, I forgot."

Clay disentangled himself from Blythe's hands. "Think it's time we went somewhere else. How about if we ride over to Wauhillau and look around? It's not that far from here."

After a pleasant ride through the blooming redbuds and dogwood trees, an old wooden watermill came into view. Ross resumed his history lesson. "That's the Bidding Springs Mill. Folks say it's been there since back in the days when the Cherokees first arrived. A white doctor named Bitting rebuilt it after it was torn down the first time, but it's been fixed up and owned by different men over the years. Heard it was first called 'Bitting' after the doctor, but somehow the name changed to 'Bidding' over the years."

Bonita was thawing out. "It's sure pretty. Can we go inside?"

Ross pulled back on the reins and helped her down. "Pa brought me and Clay here once. Remember, Clay, when Pa brought us here after he looked at some horses at the Christies?"

"Yeah, I remember. He said the Christies always want too much for their horses."

The friendly miller showed them around the mill and told them more about its history.

When they got ready to go, Blythe put her hand on Clay's arm and said, "Clay, would you mind buyin' me a loaf of that fresh bread they're sellin'? I brought some of my ma's apple butter that would go real good on it for our picnic lunch."

"Sure. Here you go, ma'am." Clay handed the miller's wife a dime.

"Thank you, young man. Enjoy your bread."

"Come on, girls. We can walk to Ned's Fort from here."

After a short, uphill hike, Bonita surveyed the remains of a what looked like a burned cabin. "Why do they call it a fort? This just looks like what's left of a cabin that burned down."

"This was Ned Christie's home that he turned into a fort to try to protect himself and his family from the U.S. Marshals that Judge Parker sent to capture him."

Bonita spoke up. "Finally, Ross, I know somethin' about what you're talkin' about. Pa told me about Judge Parker. He was called the Hangin' Judge, right?"

"That's right. What did your pa say about him?"

"That he was a self-righteous old so and so who tried to see how many men he could hang."

Clay shook his head. "Grandpa Clay said somethin' different. He said Judge Parker and his marshals brought order to a lawless place.

He said Granny Bluebird spoke well of Marshal Bass Reeves and was grateful to him because he helped them out with some outlaws a long time ago."

"Your grandpa was probably closer to the truth. Pa seems to always favor the outlaw. Still, they shouldn't have burned a man's house down."

Ross regained control of the conversation. "Parker was dead wrong where Ned was concerned. Any Cherokee will tell you that Ned was framed for Deputy Marshal Dan Maples' murder. The marshals stayed after him for over five years, and they burned his house down and blinded him in one eye. Still didn't get him until they brought in a cannon and dynamite. You remember what happened next, Clay?"

"Yeah, Grandpa said they riddled him with bullets, tied his body to a door, and showed him off like a trophy. Said he saw Ned's corpse on the front steps of the Fort Smith Courthouse."

Blythe sniffled. "That's just awful! It must have really hurt his folks."

Ross nodded. "They still talk about it today. Do you want to see Ned's grave? The Christie Cemetery ain't far from here."

Ross linked his arm through Bonita's, and they walked a few yards from the Wauhillau Store. "I'll treat everybody to soda pops at the store on the way back."

Blythe grabbed Clay's arm to link with hers. "Good idea, Ross. I'm gettin' thirsty and hungry."

BONITA LOOKED AT the old granite tombstones. "That tall one in the middle looks like Ned's. What's that hand pointin' up mean?"

Clay removed Blythe's arm and moved closer to the grave. "Maybe that he went to Heaven?"

Ross nodded his head. "That sounds about right. Here's his pa's grave. His name was Watt Christie, and here's his ma, Lydia Thrower Christie. I heard they came over the Trail. Same as Granny Bluebird. There was some Christies who came over at a later time under John

Ross's management. I remember hearin' Katie Christie came with Granny, but her name wasn't Christie then."

Bonita pointed at one of the gravestones. "That one has a picture of a bird. What could that mean?"

Clay knelt by the grave and examined the picture. "I believe it's a dove. Maybe the person is at peace now?"

Blythe patted his cheek. "You are so smart, and I am so thirsty! How about that soda pop you promised to buy us?"

AFTER STOPPING BY the store, they walked back to the mill where they had left their horses tied to a hitching post. Tall Boy nickered a friendly greeting to them. The younger horse stomped his feet impatiently.

"Looks like Rascal needs to take manners lessons from Tall Boy." Ross grabbed Rascal's bridle. "Settle down, boy."

The group enjoyed a picnic in the cool shadow of the old mill. After they had eaten and rinsed off their few dishes in the cold spring water, they had throwing contests and skipped rocks.

Bonita asked, "Where are we goin' next?"

Ross said, "Maybe we should head back home. The sun will be going down in a couple of hours. We'll stop by Moonshiner Woods on the way there."

Clay and Bonita exchanged glances.

Clay said, "Maybe we better not, Ross."

"Why not?"

Blythe giggled. "I bet I know why not. Bonita is probably afraid we'll see her pa makin' moonshine."

"Shut up, Blythe! You know Pa's not had a drink in six months."

Blythe lowered her head in contrition. "I'm sorry. I guess I shouldn't have said that."

"No, you shouldn't."

Ross wagged his finger at Blythe. "Play nice, Blythe. How about we see how we feel when we get closer to the woods? Meanwhile, we can take in the sights on the way."

IT WAS NEARLY five o'clock by the time they arrived at the woods. Blythe was giggling and holding on to Clay.

He abruptly brought Tall Boy to a full stop. "Hush! Can't you hear that?"

Ross stopped Rascal beside him. "Sounds like girls screamin'. We better go see what's wrong."

Clay hesitated. "Sure, if it was just me and you, but we got the girls to think about."

Blythe started trembling. "Don't take us in them woods!"

"We can't just ignore them. Somebody is in trouble. Blythe, you get over here and ride behind Bonita. Tall Boy can carry me and Clay to the woods so we can see what's goin' on."

"Good idea. Bonita, the store's not far from here. You can go there and get help. Come on, Blythe, I'll help you up."

Ross made a running leap onto Tall Boy's back, Clay gave the horse his head, and they were gone.

Blythe hid her eyes. "Bonita, can you handle this wild horse?"

"I can do what I have to do. Now, hold on. I gotta settle him down first. You got any apples left from lunch?"

Blythe reached into the tow sack that was tied on to the saddle. "Here's one."

"Good boy, Rascal. Here you go. Have an apple."

Bonita stroked the horse's nose and gave him time to eat. She jerked the reins hard. "Giddy up, now, Rascal!"

AS THEY TROTTED down the road, Blythe gritted her teeth. "What are you tryin' to hide?"

"What do you mean?"

"I saw the look you and Clay gave each other. Tell me what's goin' on."

Bonita sighed. "All right. About a week ago me and Clay saw a man standin' in the woods. He threatened us and told us not to tell nobody we saw him."

"Did you tell the sheriff?"

"Pa told me not to."

"You should have anyway."

Bonita sighed. "I know that now."

WHEN THEY GOT to the store, Bonita tied up the horse, and ran in to tell her news. "Mister Stone, we heard some girls screamin' in Moonshiner Woods, and Ross and Clay went to see what was wrong."

Martha Stone clutched her heart. "Why didn't they wait until the sheriff came?"

"'Cause there might not be time to wait!" Josh grabbed the Winchester he kept behind the counter and gestured to his son Michael and some other men who were present.

"Come on, men. Mike, we'll take your truck. Martha, call the sheriff. You girls, stay here."

Martha had just got off the phone when she put her hand to her forehead. "I forgot to tell the sheriff something important!"

Blythe said, "What's that, Missus. Stone?"

"Minerva Pettibone and her friends stopped by here about an hour ago. They were riding their bikes in the direction of Moonshiner Woods. That could have been them you heard screaming."

Sometime later, Josh came back with three hysterical girls.

Martha hugged them and attempted to calm them down. "You poor things! Quick, Blythe, bring some water. Sit down on this bench and rest. Bonita, come and help."

Bonita patted the sobbing girls.

Priscilla, the minister's daughter, stood up, wringing her hands. "Why did you stop looking for Minerva? She's still in the woods with that man!"

Josh looked at her with pity in his eyes. "It will be all right, little lady. My son and grandsons and two other men are out there lookin' for her, and here comes the sheriff and his deputies. They'll find her in no time." Josh stepped outside to tell the sheriff what he had seen in the woods.

When he came back in, Martha stopped him. "Are the boys all right? Why didn't you bring them back with you?"

"They're fine, Martha. They wanted to show the others where the girls last saw the man and the Pettibone girl. Now, go and call the Pettibone girl's aunt, the Widow Whitmire. She has a phone, so tell her what happened. Try not to worry her. I need to get these young ladies home before their folks get to frettin' about them. Blythe, can you come along with me? I'll drop you off, too. Bonita, would you mind stayin' a little longer and helpin' Martha out. I'll stop by and tell your pa what is goin' on."

By the time Josh got back, it was completely dark, and the store was filling up with people. Martha set up kerosene lamps and lanterns throughout the store.

Minerva's aunt arrived in an agitated state. "I can't get in touch with Minerva's mother! She's somewhere in Germany and isn't due to call until tomorrow. She calls every Sunday afternoon to check on Minerva. Oh, what am I going to tell her when she calls?"

Several neighborhood men, toting guns and flashlights, arrived to join the hunt.

Anderson and Ramona came in with them, and Anderson walked over to where Bonita was sitting and gave her a bear hug. "Thank God, you're safe! Didn't I tell you to stay out of them woods?"

"I never went in them, Pa. The boys sent Blythe and me to the store while they went in."

"Well, at least they showed some sense about that."

"You need to come on home with Mona and me. There's nothin' else you can do, and Martha's got plenty of help now."

She pulled away. "I want to stay, Pa. I need to know Ross and the others are all right."

Ramona spoke up. "I'll stay, too, Mr. McKindle. I noticed Ross's horse is goin' crazy with all the traffic around here. I'll take him to the stables and take care of him."

"All right, then. If you're stayin', I'll stay too, until you're both ready to come home with me."

In about an hour, some of the search party came back. When Bonita saw Ross and Clay, she ran over and hugged them both. She looked at their grim faces and knew the news wasn't good. Ross motioned for her to follow him outside, and Clay went over to where his grandma was serving soup and crackers.

They sat down on a wooden bench on the front porch, away from the milling crowd. "We found them three girls just a few minutes after you left. They was cryin' and screamin' and runnin' around in circles. They kept sayin' that a man grabbed Minerva and ran off with her. They wouldn't stay by theirselves, so Clay stayed with them until Grandpa came. I struck out in the direction they told me he took her, but I didn't see anything for a long time. Finally, I saw some tracks by a stream that runs near the woods, and I showed them to the others when they got there. Looks like they crossed the branch. They wouldn't leave footprints if they walked in the water. The sheriff said he didn't want to be responsible for underage kids and made us leave. He kept Pa and some of the more able-bodied men with him and the deputies. Pa was arguin' with him when we left, so I have a feelin' we might be goin' back later."

"Do you think they'll find Minerva?"

"I don't know. It's mighty dark in them woods, especially at night, with no moon and only a few lanterns and flashlights to light the way. I look for the sheriff to give up the search and start again when it's daylight. Heard him say somethin' about gettin' a piece of clothin' that belonged to Minerva and bringin' some huntin' dogs in to look for her in the mornin'."

"Will it be in time?"

"Can't say. Hope so. We're goin' home so we can tell Ma what's goin' on and where Pa is. Do you know where Rascal is?"

"Ramona put him in your grandpa's stable."

"That's good. Do you need us to take you and Ramona home first?"

"No, Pa will drive us home."

Ross took a couple of steps away but stopped and turned around to face Bonita. "Clay told Pa about the man him and you saw last week. Why didn't you tell me?"

"I don't know. I probably would have, but Pa told me not to tell the sheriff or nobody."

Ross's eyes were black and cold. "I didn't like the idea of you havin' a secret with my brother that you wouldn't tell me."

She walked over and placed her hand on his arm. "I was wrong. I'm sorry."

Ross patted her hand. "I guess I forgive you, but don't ever do it again. I'll probably see you tomorrow." He gave her a quick kiss and walked away.

Anderson insisted that Bonita and Ramona eat some hot soup before he took them home. Even though she was hungry, she barely managed to get a bowl down.

On the way home, the car was quiet until Anderson cleared his throat. "Bonita, I'm sorry I told you to keep what you saw in the woods to yourself."

"I'm sorry, too. If I had told the sheriff, he might have arrested the man before he took Minerva."

"I just thought it was a moonshiner or maybe a friendly crook. I didn't imagine it was some kind of crazy man who would hurt little girls."

BONITA SLEPT FITFULLY and woke up when the first sunrays touched her bedroom window. She got up, made and ate a light breakfast, and took a quick sponge bath before getting ready in a hurry.

Anderson was still snoring, but Ramona got up and caught her before she left. "Are you goin' to the store?"

"Yeah."

"It's not open on Sundays, is it?"

"I think it will be today. People will be there to keep up with what is happenin'."

"Remember we're supposed to be at church with your granny today?"

"That's right, but I can't go. Why don't you go ahead and tell Grandma what's happenin'?"

"All right, but I'm not goin' home with her for dinner. I'll come home right after church."

"Suit yourself, but you might as well go. You know she'll have extra food cooked, and she'll want someone to help her eat it."

Ramona touched her shoulder. "Are you sure you don't need me?"

"No, I'll be all right. Just tell Pa where I'm goin' or leave a note if he's asleep when you leave."

"All right. I'll bring you some food home."

Bonita tried to smile. "You do that."

AS SHE WALKED to the store, she heard the welcome sound of baying hounds.

Amelia Stone and her family were at the store, along with several Jubilee inhabitants. She and some of the other women of the community had brought food in for the search party. Bonita spotted Martha, giving orders to Emily to "handle the cash register."

She asked, "Is there anything you need me to do, Missus Stone?"

"Thanks, dear. You might ask Emily if she needs any help minding the store."

Emily said, "Sure. I could use some help. Keep your eye on the kiddies. I think they're tryin' to sneak peanuts out of the barrel when their mamas aren't lookin'. Just stand over there, and they'll know someone is watchin' them."

Bonita walked to the peanut barrel, and the children gathered there scattered like a covey of quails. She stood there for a while, trying to look stern. After she observed the kids playing outside, she walked back to where Emily was standing.

"Any news?"

"Nothin' except Ross and Clay talked the sheriff into lettin' them help with the hunt."

"I thought he told them he wouldn't be responsible for them."

"Pa said that besides the girls, Clay was the only witness they had as to what the man looked and sounded like, and they might need him to identify him. He said he would take full responsibility for Clay and Ross."

Bonita spent the morning helping Emily and listening to the bits of conversation that were circling about her. Minerva's aunt, the Widow Whitmire, was the center of attention, and every time she said, "I don't know what I am going to tell her mother," someone would pat her hand.

Once, she heard Amelia Stone tell her, "Perhaps you won't have to tell her anything because Minerva will be found by then. You can let Minerva tell her mother what happened herself."

Around noon, some of the search party returned to eat lunch. Bonita overheard Martha say to Amelia, "Wonder why Michael and the boys didn't come and eat? You know they must be hungry. They've been at it since daylight."

"I packed some food for them to carry with them."

SOME OF THE party were still there when the sheriff's car pulled up and parked. All talking ceased and every eye was upon him when he walked into the store. Bonita noticed his hands were trembling as he pulled off his Stetson and walked over to address Julia Whitmire.

"I'm sorry, ma'am."

The women sitting nearby caught her before she crumpled to the floor in a faint. Josh and another man stepped forward and carried her to a small cot he kept in the back of the store.

The sheriff put on his hat and turned to face the crowd. "You folks can go home now. Miss Minerva's body has been found."

A huge, freckled, red-haired man, shaking with pent-up emotion, stood up and faced the sheriff. "And the scum who murdered her?"

"Dead."

The man nodded. "That's good. Saves me the trouble." He sat back down where he had been sitting.

The sheriff walked to the counter and spoke to Martha. "Martha, when she comes to, would you tell the Widow I will be takin' her niece's body to the county coroner? When he's finished, I will let her know when she can be buried. She probably needs to get ahold of the girl's mother as soon as she can."

"I'll tell her."

THE SHERIFF LEFT, and the talking resumed. Bonita heard one man say, "The sheriff done wrong by callin' off the hunt last night. He might have saved the girl if he hadn't quit."

Another remark cut her to the heart. "I heard tell one of the Stone boys seen the man in the woods last week. Seen him and said nothin'! I say that girl's blood is on his hands!" Several men agreed with this remark, and an angry buzz filled the room.

Michael, Clay, and Ross walked into the store and were surrounded. The red-haired man confronted them.

"Which of them boys caused that girl to die?"

Stone-faced, Michael pointed his rifle at the man. "Neither one of them. Now you back off!"

Josh brought out his Winchester and stepped behind him. "You heard my son. Get out of my store!"

Amelia Stone came forward and stood beside him with a revolver in her hand.

Bonita couldn't believe her eyes. She had never imagined Amelia Stone as a woman familiar with guns, but the look in her flat, black eyes reminded her of a mama bear determined to defend her cubs.

The red-haired man and his followers turned around and stalked from the store, making obscene gestures, and pushing their way through the crowd that had gathered behind them. After they left, Josh lowered his weapon and addressed the crowd.

"Now, folks, I didn't recognize that man who just left, but I know most all of you here, and you are all good people. Me and my family have always been law-abiding citizens. Now, one of my grandsons made a foolish mistake, but he didn't do it out of malice. He kept his mouth shut out of fear. The man threatened to hurt him and the girl who was with him if they told anyone he was there. The boy didn't realize what kind of man he was dealin' with. He thought he was just a bootlegger or a small-time crook. If he had knowed what the man was capable of, he would have gone straight to the sheriff. We all know kids make mistakes on their way to growin' up, and all we can do is try to set them right." Josh paused and smiled. "Well, today is Sunday, but I didn't mean to preach. Bein' that it's Sunday, the store is closed. Let's all go home and pray for the family who lost one of their children."

Bonita hid away when the crowd left the store. She noticed Ross and Clay looked pale and sick. Michael hugged his boys, and Amelia patted their shoulders. Ross stayed in his father's embrace, but Clay walked over to Josh.

"Thanks, Grandpa." He gathered the small man in his big arms.

"You're welcome, boy." Josh stepped back and wiped the tears from his eyes.

BONITA WENT OUTSIDE and waited for Clay and Ross to leave the store. When she saw them emerge, she pulled them aside.

"Thanks for not mentionin' my name. It was really more my fault than yours, Clay. I talked you out of goin' to the sheriff." She fought to hold back tears.

Ross held her as Clay said, "Neither of us knew what was goin' to happen, just like Grandpa said."

VIII
FAREWELLS

AFTER THE AUTOPSY, Widow Whitmire sent Minerva's body to Tulsa for an elaborate funeral. Minerva's three friends from Jubilee attended with their parents. The mother of one of the girls came to the store the day after the funeral and gave the crowd a full report. Minerva's mother, her father, her grandparents, and other relatives, all elegantly attired, sat "as still as statues" throughout the service but "talked plenty afterwards."

At the funeral meal, all conversations centered around the tragedy and the general worthlessness of the sheriff and the citizens of Jubilee. Widow Whitmire reportedly said she had made arrangements with her lawyer to sell the house and property she owned, and she knew she would be much happier living with her own kind in Tulsa.

Martha Stone said, "Horse Feathers! If her mother had kept Minerva with her, that poor girl would still be alive. And as for the widow, if she thinks she's too good to live with the folks around here, then we're glad to see her go."

For once everyone agreed with her.

BONITA STRUGGLED WITH the desire to ask Ross for the details of Minerva's murder. Finally, she got her nerve up and approached him when they were talking after school.

"Ross, I would like to know what happened in the woods."

Ross sighed, bit his lip, and stared at the floor for several minutes. He looked up, took a deep breath, and started talking. "All right. I think I can talk about it. The hounds picked up the scent on the other side of the branch that ran through the woods. It took them some time, and they lost it a time or two."

He stopped and looked away before resuming talking. "I spotted her first. She was layin' back in the corner of a cave, naked, and covered with blood. The coroner said later she had been raped before she was stabbed."

She pulled Ross close to her. She could feel his body trembling. "That's awful!"

"It was an awful thing to see. What happened next was almost as bad."

"You mean when the sheriff killed the murderer?"

"The sheriff didn't kill him. Pa did."

Bonita pulled back and stared at his face. "What?"

"It happened like this. He came runnin' at Clay with a long knife in his hand, hollerin', 'I told you not to come back!' Pa blew him away with his rifle. "

Ross looked away for a minute before he resumed speaking. "The sheriff heard the commotion and saw what had happened. He said it was self-defense. They buried him in the Jubilee Cemetery in an unmarked grave."

"Well, I'm glad to know exactly what happened, even if it was awful."

"Yeah, Clay is still havin' nightmares about it. I think he blames hisself for Minerva's death."

Bonita wiped her eyes. "He's not the only one."

Ross gave her a handkerchief and kissed her forehead. "Now, you got to quit thinkin' like that. There's nothin' you can do to undo what happened. You just got to get on with your life and be happy."

"I'll try."

"And I'll help you, darlin'." Ross kissed her again, deeply this time.

A WEEK LATER, Bonita was out of groceries, so she walked to the Stone Store. Emily was sweeping off the front porch, but when she spotted Bonita, she put her broom down and started chatting. They had only talked for a few minutes when Martha yelled out the front door.

"Emily, I need your help in here! I can't do everything by myself!"

"All right, Granny. Just a minute. Hey, before I go, why don't you come to church tomorrow? We're having a baptizin', and most of the family's getting baptized."

"In the creek, this time of year? Bet that water's goin' to be cold!"

"Probably so, but Ma says it's time she gets baptized, and she wants all of us that are saved in the family to be baptized with her. We're all getting baptized except for Pa, Ross, and the little ones. Oh, and Susan because she's pregnant, and it might hurt the baby."

"Even Clay?"

"Especially Clay. He's been moody ever since Minerva was killed. He got saved at the revival last week. So did all of us girls. Ma says she's been saved for years, but it's time for her to make it public by being baptized. After the baptizing, the church will have dinner on the ground."

"I don't know. I haven't gone much since I quit livin' with Grandma."

"Your Granny will probably be there. Why don't you and Ramona come?"

"Ramona is sick again, but I'll try to come. Maybe I can use Sid's bicycle to get there."

"Good! See you tomorrow."

THE NEXT MORNING, Bonita hurried from bed, dressed, and found an old pair of Sid's jeans to wear under her dress. That would keep nosey folks from seeing her drawers. She had asked Ramona if she felt like coming the night before.

"I better not. I'm still coughin' my head off. I'll just stay here with your pa. He's feelin' puny too, but I bet he would appreciate any food you could bring home."

"I'll take a flour sack and see if I can carry some food home for both of you."

A little over an hour later, she arrived at the small, white country church, just a little late. After she parked the bike near the front porch, she jumped when she heard a hiss coming from the bushes.

"Psst! I thought that was you. Why don't you join me in the bushes instead of goin' to sit with all of them church folks? We would have more fun in the bushes than you can have with them respectable hypocrites."

"Shame on you, Ross Stone! I came to watch your family get baptized. Now I can see why they wouldn't want to baptize you. You've been drinkin', haven't you?"

"So what if I have? It's a lot more fun than sittin' with all of them church people. If you would try it, maybe you would loosen up, and me and you could have lots of fun."

"No, thank you. I don't like bein' around drunks, and I came here to go to church, and that's what I'm goin' to do."

He tipped up the brown jug and took another nip. "Oh, well, suit yourself. If you get too bored, you know where to find me."

Bonita squeezed into a crowded pew right behind where her grandma was sitting.

Grandma smiled when she saw Bonita. "There's my girl! I'm so glad to see you back in the Lord's House again."

"I'm glad to be here, Grandma. I've been missin' this place and you."

Bonita looked over the heads of all the people and spotted Emily and her family, sitting on the third row. They were all there, except Ross, and they were all smiling, even the usually solemn-faced Amelia. What would it be like to have a normal happy family with a father, a mother, brothers, and sisters?

SHE STOOD BY Grandma during the baptisms and joined the congregation as they gave the right hand of fellowship to those who were newly baptized.

"Glad you came, Bonita," said Clay, and he squeezed her hand as he shook it.

As he walked away, Grandma began whispering. "I think that Stone boy is sweet on you."

"You mean Clay? I suppose he is, but his brother is better lookin' and a good dancer."

"Looks ain't that important. I heard tell that Ross Stone is already a drinker."

"I think he is. Oh, well, I don't have to marry him. I just like to look at him and dance with him a little."

"Just be careful, Nita. That's kinda like what your ma said about your pa. She claimed she was bein' nice to him because he was a nice lookin', lonely gentleman. Look what that got her."

"Suppose you're right, Grandma. Don't worry. I know better than to make her mistake."

"I hope so. You need to let Ross go and latch on to his big brother."

"I'll think about what you said."

The church ladies packed Bonita's sack full of fried chicken, biscuits, ham slices, and even some of Amelia Stone's delicious fried pies. It had been a very good day.

ABOUT A MONTH later, Bonita and Ramona came home from school, laughing and teasing each other about things that had happened at school that day. When they opened the front door, Bonita's gut turned and twisted. The old signs were there, dirty dishes piled in the sink and vomit and excrement on the kitchen floor.

"Pa's drinkin' again! He's been doin' so good. Wonder what set him off?" Scanning the room, she saw Sid's familiar suitcase by Ramona's bed. "That explains it. Sid is back."

"Your brother?"

"Yeah. It won't do no good to try to run him off. Pa will just say he's welcome."

Ramona's shoulders shook as she swallowed her tears. Bonita patted her on the back and gave her a big hug. "It will be all right, Ramona. We'll figure out something."

Ramona stepped back and looked Bonita squarely in the face. "No, it won't ever be all right again. Guess I better find me another place to live."

"You don't have to leave."

"Yes, I do. Sid already claimed my bed, and he'll want me gone, or else he'll try to bother me like my brothers. I can't stand that no more. Time to go to Tulsa and start my new life. I got eighty dollars for my bus ticket, room, and food. That will run me till I get my first paycheck."

"Before you go, let me look for Pa's stash. He used to hide money to keep anyone from gettin' it. But he would always get drunk and forget where he hid it." Bonita began to search the small house.

"Well, here's the sugar bowl, but it don't have nothin' in it. He must have hid it somewhere else." She opened an old coffee can that was hidden in the back of the cabinet. "Here it is. Let's see how much."

Bonita dumped the can out and counted. "Almost twenty-five dollars in change and bills."

"I got plenty already for transportation and everything else until I get paid from the job I'll get. You might need that money. Are you sure you want to give it all to me?"

"Never surer. In the mornin', instead of walkin' to school, you can walk to Tahlequah and catch a bus. More than likely you won't have to walk the whole way because somebody will come along you can hitch a ride from."

"Where will I stay tonight?"

"You can stay here. They're probably gone on a long bender."

"All right. Let me help you clean up the mess."

BONITA HUGGED RAMONA the next morning right before she set off walking to Tahlequah. "Remember to write me now? I'll be worryin' until I hear."

"How about you? What are you gonna do?"

"Just keep on livin' here like before until I find a way out. Maybe I'll save up my money and catch a bus like you are doin'."

"If you do, you can live with me."

"Well, I just might. Bye, Ramona. I'm goin' to miss you!"

"I'll miss you too, Bonita! I better go before I start cryin'. Bye."

She stood on the front porch and watched her friend walk toward Tahlequah, suitcase in hand. She watched Ramona until she couldn't see her anymore. Then she wiped her eyes and went back inside to get ready for her own walk to school.

THE NEW HISTORY teacher, Miss Swepston, asked Bonita why Ramona hadn't come to school with her that day.

Bonita just grinned and replied, "Oh, you know, she is a Freedle, and you never know what a Freedle might do." Bonita was praying with all her soul that her friend had escaped.

"That's so disappointing! I wasn't surprised when her brothers quit school, but Ramona seemed to be doing so well. If you ever hear from her, tell her Miss Swepston misses her and wishes she would come back to school."

"I will tell her that very thing if I hear from her, Miss Swepston."

TWO WEEKS LATER, when Bonita got a letter postmarked from Tulsa, she could hardly wait to tear it open.

> *Dear Bonita*
>
> *Well I done did it. I'm livin in Tulsa now and have got a fine job in a cannin factry. I have a aparment of my on with my on ice box, stove, and bed. I even got a inside tolet and a big bathtub. Come and see me sometime.*
>
> *Your Friend Fourever*
> *Ramona*

Bonita sat quietly, staring at the letter, planning her own escape.

AUTHOR'S NOTE

CHEROKEE STONE, MY second book, was actually the core of the first book that I wrote. It was roughly based on my Cherokee grandmother's experience of being sent to a mission school to live when her mother passed away. I began the book with the protagonist, Amelia, being left at a mission school and then continued her life story and the stories of her relatives, friends, and acquaintances.

Before I say anything else, I must claim the author's right to poetic license. Although my books may be roughly inspired by real people and events, most of the more dramatic details are strictly products of my own imagination.

After I retired and began researching Cherokee history and my Cherokee genealogy, I revised the book to begin at the Removal and added additional characters and much more history.

During the process of working with my publisher, Oghma Creative Media, my editor convinced me to expand my one book, which covered over 150 years, into a series. Now I have completed the series, "Cherokee Passages," which consists of three books: *Cherokee Clay*, *Cherokee Stone*, and *Cherokee Steel*. Historical and genealogical research, as well as interviewing some of the elders of my family, provided ideas for story development.

Once again, I want to thank the editors and staff members of Oghma. They have served as my teachers, critics, and supporters all the way through the development of my three novels. Now I can enjoy the fruits of my labor, watching others read what I have written.

9 781633 737037